Practice Book

Leland Powers

Contents

PRACTICE BOOK

BY

Leland Powers

IN ACKNOWLEDGMENT.

My gratitude to publishers who have generously permitted the reprinting of copyrighted selections, I would here publicly express. To Little, Brown & Company I am indebted for the use of the extract called "Eloquence," which is taken from a discourse by Daniel Webster; to Small, Maynard & Company for the poem "A Conservative," taken from a volume by Mrs. Gilman, entitled "In This Our World;" to the Lothrop, Lee & Shepard Company for the poems by Mr. Burton; and to Longmans, Green & Company for the extracts from the works of John Ruskin. The selections from Sill and Emerson are used by permission of, and by special arrangement with, Houghton, Mifflin & Company, publishers of their works.

The quotations under the headings "Exercises for Elemental Vocal Expression" and "Exercises for Transition," with a few exceptions, are taken from "The Sixth Reader," by the late Lewis B. Monroe, and are here reprinted through the courtesy of the American Book Company.

LELAND POWERS.

INDEX

EXERCISES FOR ELEMENTAL VOCAL EXPRESSION.

The exercises under each chapter have **primarily** the characteristics of that chapter, and **secondarily** the characteristics of the other two chapters.

CHAPTER I.
VITALITY.

MIND ACTIVITIES DOMINATED BY A CONSCIOUSNESS OF *Power, Largeness, Freedom, Animation, Movement*.

1. "Ho! strike the flag-Staff deep, Sir Knight--ho! scatter flowers, fair
      maids:
   Ho! gunners, fire a loud salute--ho! gallants, draw your blades."

2. "Awake, Sir King, the gates unspar!
   Rise up and ride both fast and far!
   The sea flows over bolt and bar."

3. "I would call upon all the true sons of New England to co-operate with
the laws of man and the justice of heaven."

4. "Robert of Sicily, brother of Pope Urbane,
   And Volmond, emperor of Allemaine,
   Apparelled in magnificent attire,
   With retinue of many a knight and squire,
   On St. John's eve at vespers proudly sat,
   And heard the priest chant the Magnificat."

5. "Then the master,
   With a gesture of command,
   Waved his hand;
   And at the word,
   Loud and sudden there was heard
   All around them and below
   The sound of hammers, blow on blow,
   Knocking away the shores and spurs.
   And see! she stirs!
   She starts,--she moves,--she seems to feel
   The thrill of life along her keel,
   And, spurning with her foot the ground,
   With one exulting, joyous bound,
   She leaps into the ocean's arms!"

6. "Under his spurning feet, the road
   Like an arrowy Alpine river flowed,
   And the landscape sped away behind,
   Like an ocean flying before the wind."

7. "The wind, one morning sprang up from sleep,
   Saying, 'Now for a frolic! now for a leap!
   Now for a madcap galloping chase!
   I'll make a commotion in every place!'"

8. "O hark! O hear! how thin and clear,
   And thinner, clearer, farther going!
   O sweet and far, from cliff and scar,
   The horns of Elfland faintly blowing!"

9. "It is done!
   Clang of bell and roar of gun!
   Send the tidings up and down.

How the belfries rock and reel!
How the great guns, peal on peal,
Fling the joy from town to town!"

10. "O sacred forms, how proud you look!
How high you lift your heads into the sky!
How huge you are, how mighty and how free!
Ye are the things that tower, that shine; whose smile
Makes glad--whose frown is terrible; whose forms,
Robed or unrobed, do all the impress wear
Of awe divine."

CHAPTER II.
MENTALITY.

MIND ACTIVITIES DOMINATED BY A CONSCIOUSNESS OF *Reflection*
OR
Processes OF *Thought, Clearness, Definiteness*.

1. "Beyond the street a tower,--beyond the tower a moon,--beyond the moon
a star,--beyond the Star, what?"

2. "Once more: speak clearly, if you speak at all;
   Carve every word before you let it fall;
   Don't, like a lecturer or dramatic star,
   Try overhard to roll the British R;
   Do put your accents in the proper spot;
   Don't--let me beg you--don't say 'How?' for 'What?'
   And when you stick on conversation's burrs,
   Don't strew the pathway with those dreadful urs."

3. "To be, or not to be; that is the question:--
   Whether 'tis nobler in the mind to suffer
   The slings and arrows of outrageous fortune;
   Or to take arms against a sea of troubles,
   And by opposing end them? To die: to sleep,--

No more:"

4. "I should say sincerity, a deep, great, genuine sincerity, is the first characteristic of all men in any way heroic. Not the sincerity that calls itself sincere; that is ... oftenest self-conceit mainly. The great man's sincerity is of the kind he cannot speak of, is not conscious of."

5. "Brutus. Get me a taper in my study, Lucius.

Lucius. I will, my lord. (Exit.)

Brutus. It must be by his death: and for my part,
I know no cause to spurn at him,
But for the general. He would be crown'd:--
How that might change his nature, there's the question.
It is the bright day that brings forth the adder;
And that craves wary walking. Crown him?--That:--
And then, I grant, we put a sting in him,
That at his will he may do danger with."

6. "In the beginning was the Word, and the Word was with God, and the Word was God. The same was in the beginning with God."

7. "Just in proportion as the writer's aim, consciously or unconsciously, comes to be the transcribing, not of the world, not of mere fact, but of his sense of it, he becomes an artist; his work a *fine* art, and good art in proportion to the truth of his presentment of that sense. Truth! there can be no merit, no craft at all, without that. And further, all beauty is in the long run only *fineness* of truth, or what we call expression, the finer accommodation of speech to that vision within."

8. "For the Universe has three children, born at one time, which reappear, under different names, in every system of thought, whether they be called

cause, operation, and effect; or, theologically, the Father, the Spirit, and the Son; but which we call here, the Knower, the Doer, and the Sayer. These stand respectively for the love of truth, for the love of good, and for the love of beauty. These three are equal. Each of these three has the power of the others latent in him, and his own patent."

CHAPTER III.
MORALITY.

MIND ACTIVITIES DOMINATED BY A CONSCIOUSNESS OF *Purpose, Love, Harmony,*
Poise, Values.

1. "My friend, if thou hadst all the artillery of Woolwich trundling at thy back in support of an unjust thing, and infinite bonfires visibly waiting ahead of thee, to blaze centuries long for thy victory on behalf of it, I would advise thee to call halt, to fling down thy baton, and say, 'In Heaven's name, No!'"

2. "Flower in the crannied wall,
    I pluck you out of the crannies;--
Hold you here, root and all, in my hand,
    Little flower--but if I could understand
What you are, root and all, and all in all,
    I should know what God and man is."

3. "Who but the locksmith could have made such music? A gleam of sun shining through the unsashed window and checkering the dark workshop with

a broad patch of light fell full upon him, as though attracted by his sunny heart."

4. "Portia You see me, Lord Bassanio, where I stand,
   Such as I am; though for myself alone,
   I would not be ambitious in my wish,
   To wish myself much better; yet, for you,
   I would be trebled twenty times myself;
   A thousand times more fair, ten thousand times more rich;"

5. "Listen to the water-mill;
   Through the livelong day,
   How the clicking of its wheels
   Wears the hours away!
   Languidly the autumn wind
   Stirs the forest leaves,
   From the fields the reapers sing,
   Binding up their sheaves;
   And a proverb haunts my mind,
   As a spell is cast;
   'The mill can never grind
   With the water that is past.'"

6. "Roaming in thought over the Universe, I saw the little that is good steadily hastening towards immortality. And the vast all that is called evil I saw hastening to merge itself, and become lost and dead."

7. "We one day descried some shapeless object drifting at a distance. At sea, everything that breaks the monotony of the surrounding expanse attracts attention. It proved to be the mast of a ship that must have been completely wrecked; for there were the remains of handkerchiefs, by which some of the crew had fastened themselves to this spar, to prevent their being washed off by the waves.

"There was no trace by which the name of the ship could be ascertained. The wreck had evidently drifted about for many months; clusters of shell-fish had fastened about it, and long sea-weeds flaunted at its sides. But where, thought I, are the crew? Their struggle has long been over. They have gone down amidst the roar of the tempest. Their bones lie whitening among the caverns of the deep. Silence, oblivion, like the waves, have closed over them, and no one can tell the story of their end."

8. "Sunset and evening star, and one clear call for me!
   And may there be no moaning of the bar when I put out to sea;
   But such a tide as moving seems asleep, too full for sound and foam,
   When that which drew from out the boundless deep turns again home."

9. "Lord, thou hast been our dwelling-place in all generations. Before the mountains were brought forth, or ever thou hadst formed the earth and the world, even from everlasting to everlasting, thou art God."

EXERCISES FOR TRANSITION.

1. "O, how our organ can speak with its many and wonderful voices!--
   Play on the soft lute of love, blow the loud trumpet of war,
   Sing with the high sesquialtro, or, drawing its full diapason,
   Shake all the air with the grand storm of its pedals and stops."

2. "The combat deepens. On, ye brave,
   Who rush to glory or the grave!
   Wave, Munich! all thy banners wave,
     And charge with all thy chivalry!

"Ah! few shall part where many meet!
 The snow shall be their winding sheet,
 And every turf beneath their feet
   Shall be a soldier's sepulcher."

3. "Lo, dim in the starlight their white tents appear!
   Ride softly! ride slowly! the onset is near
   More slowly! more softly! the sentry may hear!
   Now fall on the foe like a tempest of flame!
   Strike down the false banner whose triumph were shame!
   Strike, strike for the true flag, for freedom and fame!"

4. "Hush! hark! did stealing steps go by?
   Came not faint whispers near?
   No!--The wild wind hath many a sigh
   Amid the foliage sere."

5.   "Her giant form
   O'er wrathful surge, through blackening storm,
   Majestically calm, would go,
   Mid the deep darkness, white as snow!
   But gentler now the small waves glide,
   Like playful lambs o'er a mountain's side.
   So stately her bearing, so proud her array,
   The main she will traverse for ever and aye.
   Many ports will exult at the gleam of her mast.
   Hush! hush! thou vain dreamer! this hour is her last!"

6. "Hark! distant voices that lightly
   Ripple the silence deep!
   No; the swans that, circling nightly,
   Through the silver waters sweep.

"See I not, there, a white shimmer?
Something with pale silken shrine?
No; it is the column's glimmer,
'Gainst the gloomy hedge of pine."

7. "Hark, below the gates unbarring!
   Tramp of men and quick commands!
   ''Tis my lord come back from hunting,'
   And the Duchess claps her hands.

   "Slow and tired came the hunters;
   Stopped in darkness in the court.
   'Ho, this way, ye laggard hunters!
   To the hall! What sport, what sport.'

   "Slow they entered with their master;
   In the hall they laid him down.
   On his coat were leaves and blood-stains,
   On his brow an angry frown."

8. "Now clear, pure, hard, bright, and one by one, like to hailstones,
   Short words fall from his lips fast as the first of a shower,--
   Now in twofold column, Spondee, Iamb, and Trochee,
   Unbroke, firm-set, advance, retreat, trampling along,--
   Now with a sprightlier springiness, bounding in triplicate syllables,
   Dance the elastic Dactylics in musical cadences on;
   Now, their voluminous coil intertangling like huge anacondas,
   Roll overwhelmingly onward the sesquipedalian words."

SELECTIONS.

HERVE RIEL.

On the sea and at the Hogue, sixteen hundred ninety-two,
Did the English fight the French,--woe to France!
And the thirty-first of May, helter-skelter through the blue,
Like a crowd of frightened porpoises a shoal of sharks pursue,
Came crowding ship on ship to Saint Malo on the Rance,
  With the English fleet in view.

'Twas the squadron that escaped, with the victor in full chase;
First and foremost of the drove, in his great ship, Damfreville;
      Close on him fled, great and small,
      Twenty-two good ships in all;
      And they signalled to the place,
      "Help the winners of a race!
Get us guidance, give us harbor, take us quick--or quicker still,
      Here's the English can and will!"

Then the pilots of the place put out brisk and leapt on board;
"Why, what hope or chance have ships like these to pass?" laughed they:
"Rocks to starboard, rocks to port, all the passage scarred and scored,
Shall the 'Formidable' here with her twelve and eighty guns,
Think to make the river-mouth by the single narrow way,
Trust to enter where 'tis ticklish for a craft of twenty tons,
      And with flow at full beside?
      Now 'tis slackest ebb of tide.

Reach the mooring? Rather say,
    While rock stands or water runs,
    Not a ship will leave the bay!"

Then was called a council straight.
    Brief and bitter the debate:
"Here's the English at our heels; would you have them take in tow
All that's left us of the fleet, linked together stern and bow,
    For a prize to Plymouth Sound?--
    Better run the ships aground!"
    (Ended Damfreville his speech.)
    "Not a minute more to wait!
    Let the captains all and each
Shove ashore, then blow up, burn the vessels on the beach!
    France must undergo her fate.
    Give the word!"--But no such word
    Was ever spoke or heard;
For up stood, for out stepped, for in struck amid all these
A captain? A lieutenant? A mate--first, second, third?
    No such man of mark, and meet
    With his betters to compete!
But a simple Breton sailor pressed by Tourville for the fleet--
A poor coasting pilot he, Herve Riel the Croisickese.

And "What mockery or malice have we here?" cries Herve Riel;
"Are you mad, you Malouins? Are you cowards, fools, or rogues?
Talk to me of rocks and shoals, me who took the soundings, tell
On my fingers every bank, every shallow, every swell,
'Twixt the offing here and Greve, where the river disembogues?
Are you bought by English gold? Is it love the lying's for?
    Morn and eve, night and day,
    Have I piloted your bay,
Entered free and anchored fast at the foot of Solidor.

Burn the fleet and ruin France? That were worse than fifty Hogues!
Sirs, they know I speak the truth! Sirs, believe me there's a way!
     Only let me lead the line,
     Have the biggest ship to steer,
     Get this 'Formidable' clear,
     Make the others follow mine,
And I lead them, most and least, by a passage I know well,
     Right to Solidor, past Greve,
     And there lay them safe and sound;
     And if one ship misbehave,--
     Keel so much as grate the ground,
Why, I've nothing but my life,--and here's my head!" cries Herve Riel.

     Not a minute more to wait.
     "Steer us in, then, small and great!
Take the helm, lead the line, save the squadron!" cried its chief.
     "Captains, give the sailor place!
     He is Admiral, in brief."
     Still the north-wind, by God's grace!
     See the noble fellow's face
     As the big ship with a bound,
     Clears the entry like a hound,
Keeps the passage as its inch of way were the wide sea's profound!
     See, safe through shoal and rock,
     How they follow in a flock.
Not a ship that misbehaves, not a keel that grates the ground,
     Not a spar that comes to grief!
     The peril, see, is past,
     All are harbored to the last,
And just as Herve Riel hollas "Anchor!"--sure as fate,
     Up the English come, too late.

So, the storm subsides to calm;
They see the green trees wave
On the heights o'erlooking Greve.
Hearts that bled are stanched with balm.
"Just our rapture to enhance,
Let the English rake the bay,
Gnash their teeth and glare askance
As they cannonade away!
Neath rampired Solidor pleasant riding on the Rance!"
Now hope succeeds despair on each captain's countenance!
Out burst all with one accord,
"This is Paradise for hell!
Let France, let France's king,
Thank the man that did the thing!"
What a shout, and all one word,
　"Herve Riel!"
As he stepped in front once more,
Not a symptom of surprise
In the frank blue Breton eyes,
Just the same man as before.

Then said Damfreville, "My friend,
I must speak out at the end,
Though I find the speaking hard.
Praise is deeper than the lips;
You have saved the King his ships,
You must name your own reward.
Faith, our sun was near eclipse!
Demand whate'er you will,
France remains your debtor still
Ask to heart's content, and have! or my name's not Damfreville!"

Then a beam of fun outbroke
On the bearded mouth that spoke,
As the honest heart laughed through
Those frank eyes of Breton blue:
"Since I needs must say my say,
Since on board the duty's done,
And from Malo roads to Croisic Point, what is it but a run?--
Since 'tis ask and have, I may--
Since the others go ashore--
Come! A good whole holiday!
Leave to go and see my wife, whom I call the Belle Aurore!"
That he asked, and that he got--nothing more.
Name and deed alike are lost:
Not a pillar nor a post
In his Croisic keeps alive the feat as it befell;
Not a head in white and black
On a single fishing-smack,
In memory of the man but for whom had gone to wrack
All that France saved from the fight whence England bore the bell.
Go to Paris; rank on rank
Search the heroes flung pell-mell
On the Louvre, face and flank!
You shall look long enough ere you come to Herve Riel.
So, for better and for worse,
Herve Riel, accept my verse!
In my verse, Herve Riel, do thou once more
Save the squadron, honor France, love thy wife, the Belle Aurore!

ROBERT BROWNING.

LOCHINVAR.

I.

Oh, young Lochinvar is come out of the West,--
Through all the wild border his steed was the best!
And, save his good broadsword, he weapon had none,--
He rode all unarmed, and he rode all alone.
So faithful in love, and so dauntless in war,
There never was knight like the young Lochinvar.

II.

He stayed not for brake, and he stopped not for stone;
He swam the Eske river where ford there was none.
But, ere he alighted at Netherby gate,
The bride had consented, the gallant came late;
For a laggard in love and a dastard in war
Was to wed the fair Ellen of brave Lochinvar.

III.

So boldly he entered the Netherby hall,
'Mong bridesmen, and kinsmen, and brothers, and all:
Then spoke the bride's father, his hand on his sword

(For the poor craven bridegroom said never a word)
"Oh, come ye in peace here, or come ye in war,
Or to dance at our bridal, young Lord Lochinvar?"

IV.

"I long wooed your daughter--my suit you denied;
Love swells like the Solway, but ebbs like its tide;
And now am I come, with this lost love of mine,
To lead but one measure, drink one cup of wine.
There are maidens in Scotland more lovely by far
That would gladly be bride to the young Lochinvar."

V.

The bride kissed the goblet; the knight took it up;
He quaffed off the wine, and he threw down the cup.
She looked down to blush, and she looked up to sigh,
With a smile on her lip and a tear in her eye.
He took her soft hand, ere her mother could bar;
"Now tread we a measure?" said young Lochinvar.

VI.

So stately his form, and so lovely her face,
That never a hall such a galliard did grace;
While her mother did fret and her father did fume,
And the bridegroom stood dangling his bonnet and plume,
And the bride-maidens whispered, "'Twere better by far
To have matched our fair cousin with young Lochinvar."

VII.

One touch to her hand and one word in her ear,
When they reached the hall door, and the charger stood near;
So light to the croup the fair lady he swung
So light to the saddle before her he sprung:
"She is won! we are gone! over bank, bush, and scar;
They'll have fleet steeds that follow," quoth young Lochinvar.

VIII.

There was mounting 'mong Graemes of the Netherby clan;
Forsters, Fenwicks, and Musgraves, they rode and they ran;
There was racing and chasing on Cannobie Lee;
But the lost bride of Netherby ne'er did they see.
So daring in love, and so dauntless in war,
Have ye e'er heard of gallant like young Lochinvar?

SIR WALTER SCOTT.

EXTRACTS FROM PIPPA PASSES.

1. "DAY."

Day!
Faster and more fast;
O'er night's brim, day boils at last:
Boils, pure gold, o'er the cloud-cup's brim
Where spurting and suppressed it lay,
For not a froth-flake touched the rim
Of yonder gap in the solid gray,
Of the eastern cloud, an hour away;
But forth one wavelet, then another curled,
Till the whole sunrise, not to be suppressed,
Rose, reddened, and its seething breast
Flickered in bounds, grew gold, then overflowed the world.
Oh Day, if I squandered a wavelet of thee,
A mite of my twelve hours' treasure,
The least of thy gazes or glances,
(Be they grants thou art bound to or gifts above measure)
One of thy choices or one of thy chances,
(Be they tasks God imposed thee or freaks at thy pleasure)
--My day, if I squander such labor or leisure,
Then shame fall on Asolo, mischief on me!

ROBERT BROWNING.

II. "THE YEAR'S AT THE SPRING."

The year's at the spring
And day's at the morn;
Morning's at seven;
The hillside's dew-pearled;
The lark's on the wing;
The snail's on the thorn:
God's in his heaven--
All's right with the world!

ROBERT BROWNING.

THE FEZZIWIG BALL.

Old Fezziwig laid down his pen, and looked up at the clock, which pointed to the hour of seven. He rubbed his hands; adjusted his capacious waistcoat; laughed all over himself, from his shoes to his organ of benevolence; and called out in a comfortable, oily, rich, fat, jovial voice: "Yo ho, there! Ebenezer! Dick!"

A living and moving picture of Scrooge's former self, a young man, came briskly in, accompanied by his fellow-prentice.

"Yo ho, my boys!" said Fezziwig. "No more work to-night. Christmas eve, Dick. Christmas, Ebenezer! Let's have the shutters up, before a man can say Jack Robinson! Clear away, my lads, and let's have lots of room here!"

Clear away! There was nothing they wouldn't have cleared away, or couldn't have cleared away, with old Fezziwig looking on. It was done in a minute. Every movable was packed off, as if it were dismissed from public life forevermore; the floor was swept and watered, the lamps were trimmed, fuel was heaped upon the fire; and the warehouse was as snug and warm and dry and bright a ball-room as you would desire to see upon a winter's night.

In came a fiddler with a music-book, and went up to the lofty desk, and made an orchestra of it, and tuned like fifty stomach-aches. In came Mrs. Fezziwig, one vast substantial smile. In came the three Miss Fezziwigs, beaming and lovable. In came the six young followers whose hearts they broke. In came all the young men and women employed in the business. In came the housemaid, with her cousin the baker. In came the cook, with her brother's particular friend, the milkman. In they all came one after another; some shyly, some boldly, some gracefully, some awkwardly, some pushing, some pulling; in they all came, anyhow and everyhow. Away they all went, twenty couple at once; hands half round and back again the other way; down the middle and up again; round and round in various stages of affectionate grouping; old top couple always turning up in the wrong place; new top couple starting off again, as soon as they got there; all top couples at last, and not a bottom one to help them. When this result was brought about, old Fezziwig, clapping his hands to Stop the dance, cried out, "Well done!" and the fiddler plunged his hot face into a pot of porter especially provided for that purpose.

There were more dances, and there were forfeits, and more dances, and there was cake, and there was negus, and there was a great piece of Cold Roast, and there was a great piece of Cold Boiled, and there were mince pies, and plenty of beer. But the great effect of the evening came after the Roast and Boiled, when the fiddler struck up "Sir Roger de Coverley." Then old Fezziwig stood out to dance with Mrs. Fezziwig. Top couple, too; with a good stiff piece of work cut out for them; three or four and twenty pair of partners, people who were not to be trifled with; people who would dance, and had no notion of walking.

But if they had been twice as many,--four times,--old Fezziwig would have been a match for them and so would Mrs. Fezziwig. As to *her*, she was worthy to be his partner in every sense of the term. A positive light appeared to issue from Fezziwig's calves. They shone in every part of the dance. You couldn't have predicted, at any given time, what would become of 'em next. And when old Fezziwig and Mrs. Fezziwig had gone all through the dance,--advance and retire, turn your partner, bow and courtesy, corkscrew, thread the needle and back again to your place,--Fezziwig "cut,"--cut so deftly, that he appeared to wink with his legs.

When the clock struck eleven this domestic ball broke up. Mr. and Mrs. Fezziwig took their stations, one on either side of the door, and, shaking hands with every person individually as he or she went out, wished him or her a Merry Christmas. When everybody had retired but the two 'prentices, they did the same to them; and thus the cheerful voices died away, and the lads were left to their beds, which were under a counter in the back shop.

THE BROOK.

I.

I come from haunts of coot and hern,
  I make a sudden sally,
And sparkle out among the fern,
  To bicker down a valley.

II.

By thirty hills I hurry down,
  Or slip between the ridges;
By twenty thorps, a little town,
  And half a hundred bridges.

III.

I chatter over stony ways,
  In little sharps and trebles,
I bubble into eddying bays,
  I babble on the pebbles.

IV.

With many a curve my banks I fret
  By many a field and fallow,
And many a fairy foreland set
  With willow-weed and mallow.

V.

I chatter, chatter, as I flow
  To join the brimming river;
For men may come, and men may go,
  But I go on forever.

VI.

I wind about and in and out,
  With here a blossom sailing,
And here and there a lusty trout,
  And here and there a grayling.

VII.

And here and there a foamy flake
  Upon me as I travel
With many a silvery water-break
  Above the golden gravel.

VIII.

I steal by lawns and grassy plots,
  I slide by hazel covers,
I move the sweet forget-me-nots
  That grow for happy lovers.

IX.

I slip, I slide, I gloom, I glance,
  Among my skimming swallows;
I make the netted sunbeam dance
  Against my sandy shallows.

X.

I murmur, under moon and stars
  In brambly wildernesses,
I linger by my shingly bars,
  I loiter round my cresses.

XI.

And out again I curve and flow
  To join the brimming river;
For men may come, and men may go,
  But I go on forever.

ALFRED, LORD TENNYSON.

A LAUGHING CHORUS.

Oh, such a commotion under the ground
  When March called, "Ho, there! ho!"
Such spreading of rootlets far and wide,
  Such whispering to and fro.
And "Are you ready?" the Snowdrop asked;
  "'Tis time to start, you know."
"Almost, my dear," the Scilla replied;
  "I'll follow as soon as you go."
Then, "Ha! ha! ha!" a chorus came
  Of laughter soft and low
From the millions of flowers under the ground--
  Yes--millions--beginning to grow.

"I'll promise my blossoms," the Crocus said,
  "When I hear the bluebirds sing."
And straight thereafter Narcissus cried,
  "My silver and gold I'll bring."
"And ere they are dulled," another spoke,
  "The Hyacinth bells shall ring."
And the violet only murmured, "I'm here,"

And sweet grew the breath of spring.
Then, "Ha! ha! ha!" a chorus came
  Of laughter soft and low
From the millions of flowers under the ground--
  Yes--millions--beginning to grow.

Oh, the pretty, brave things! through the coldest days,
  Imprisoned in walls of brown,
They never lost heart though the blast shriek loud,
  And the sleet and the hail came down,
But patiently each wrought her beautiful dress,
  Or fashioned her beautiful crown;
And now they are coming to brighten the world,
  Still shadowed by winter's frown;
And well may they cheerily laugh, "Ha! ha!"
  In a chorus soft and low,
The millions of flowers hid under the ground--
  Yes--millions--beginning to grow.

CAVALIER TUNES.

1. GIVE A ROUSE.

King Charles, and who'll do him right now?
King Charles, and who's ripe for fight now?
Give a rouse: here's, in hell's despite now,
King Charles!

Who gave me the goods that went since?
Who raised me the house that sank once?
Who helped me to gold I spent since?
Who found me in wine you drank once?

Cho. King Charles, and who'll do him right now?
        King Charles, and who's ripe for fight now?
        Give a rouse: here's, in hell's despite now,
        King Charles!

To whom used my boy George quaff else,
By the old fool's side that begot him?
For whom did he cheer and laugh else,
While Noll's damned troopers shot him.

Cho. King Charles, and who'll do him right now?
        King Charles, and who's ripe for fight now?

Give a rouse: here's, in hell's despite now,
King Charles!

II. BOOT AND SADDLE.

Boot, saddle, to horse, and away!
Rescue my castle before the hot day
Brightens to blue from its silvery gray.

Cho. Boot, saddle, to horse, and away!

Ride past the suburbs, asleep as you'd say;
Many's the friend there, will listen and pray
"God's luck to gallants that strike up the lay!"

Cho. Boot, saddle, to horse, and away!

Forty miles off, like a roebuck at bay,
Flouts Castle Brancepeth the Roundhead's array:
Who laughs, "Good fellows ere this, by my fay,

Cho. Boot, saddle, to horse, and away!"

Who? My wife Gertrude; that, honest and gay,
Laughs when you talk of surrendering, "Nay!
I've better counsellors; what counsel they?

Cho. Boot, saddle, to horse, and away!"

ROBERT BROWNING.

ACROSS THE FIELDS TO ANNE.

From Stratford-on-Avon a lane runs westward through the fields a mile to
the little village of Shottery, in which is the cottage of Anne Hathaway,
Shakespeare's sweetheart and wife.

How often in the summer tide,
His graver business set aside,
Has stripling Will, the thoughtful-eyed,
As to the pipe of Pan
Stepped blithsomely with lover's pride
Across the fields to Anne!

It must have been a merry mile,
This summer-stroll by hedge and stile,
With sweet foreknowledge all the while
How sure the pathway ran
To dear delights of kiss and smile,
Across the fields to Anne.

The silly sheep that graze to-day,
I wot, they let him go his way,
Nor once looked up, as who should say:
"It is a seemly man."
For many lads went wooing aye

Across the fields to Anne.

The oaks, they have a wiser look;
Mayhap they whispered to the brook:
"The world by him shall yet be shook,
It is in nature's plan;
Though now he fleets like any rook
Across the fields to Anne."

And I am sure, that on some hour
Coquetting soft 'twixt sun and shower,
He stooped and broke a daisy-flower
With heart of tiny span,
And bore it as a lover's dower
Across the fields to Anne.

While from her cottage garden-bed
She plucked a jasmine's goodlihede,
To scent his jerkin's brown instead;
Now since that love began,
What luckier swain than he who sped
Across the fields to Anne?

The winding path wheron I pace,
The hedgerows green, the summer's grace,
Are still before me face to face;
Methinks I almost can
Turn poet and join the singing race
Across the fields to Anne!

RICHARD BURTON.

GREEN THINGS GROWING.

The green things growing, the green things growing,
The faint sweet smell of the green things growing!
I should like to live, whether I smile or grieve,
Just to watch the happy life of my green things growing.
Oh the fluttering and the pattering of those green things growing!
How they talk each to each, when none of us are knowing;
In the wonderful white of the weird moonlight
Or the dim dreamy dawn when the cocks are crowing.
I love, I love them so--my green things growing!
And I think that they love me, without false showing;
For by many a tender touch, they comfort me so much,
With the soft mute comfort of green things growing.
And in the rich store of their blossoms glowing,
Ten for one I take they're on me bestowing:
Oh, I should like to see, if God's will it may be,
Many, many a summer of my green things growing!
But if I must be gathered for the angels' sowing,
Sleep out of sight a while like the green things growing,
Though dust to dust return, I think I'll scarcely mourn,
If I may change into green things growing.

DINAH MULOCK CRAIK.

THE TRUE USE OF WEALTH.

1. There is a saying which is in all good men's mouths; namely, that they are stewards or ministers of whatever talents are entrusted to them. Only, is it not a strange thing that while we more or less accept the meaning of that saying, so long as it is considered metaphorical, we never accept its meaning in its own terms? You know the lesson is given us under the form of a story about money. Money was given to the servants to make use of: the unprofitable servant dug in the earth, and hid his Lord's money. Well, we in our poetical and spiritual application of this, say that of course money doesn't mean money--it means wit, it means intellect, it means influence in high quarters, it means everything in the world except itself.

2. And do you not see what a pretty and pleasant come-off there is for most of us in this spiritual application? Of course, if we had wit, we would use it for the good of our fellow-creatures; but we haven't wit. Of course, if we had influence with the bishops, we would use it for the good of the church; but we haven't any influence with the bishops. Of course, if we had political power, we would use it for the good of the nation; but we have no political power; we have no talents entrusted to us of any sort or kind. It is true, we have a little money, but the parable can't possibly mean anything so vulgar as money; our money's our own.

3. I believe, if you think seriously of this matter, you will feel that the first and most literal application is just as necessary a one as any

other--that the story does very specially mean what it says--plain money; and that the reason we don't at once believe it does so, is a sort of tacit idea that while thought, wit and intellect, and all power of birth and position, are indeed given to us, and, therefore, to be laid out for the Giver,--our wealth has not been given to us; but we have worked for it, and have a right to spend it as we choose. I think you will find that is the real substance of our understanding in this matter. Beauty, we say, is given by God--it is a talent; strength is given by God--it is a talent; but money is proper wages for our day's work--it is not a talent, it is a due. We may justly spend it on ourselves, if we have worked for it.

4. And there would be some shadow of excuse for this, were it not that the very power of making the money is itself only one of the applications of that intellect or strength which we confess to be talents. Why is one man richer than another? Because he is more industrious, more persevering, and more sagacious. Well, who made him more persevering and more sagacious than others? That power of endurance, that quickness of apprehension, that calmness of judgment, which enable him to seize opportunities that others lose, and persist in the lines of conduct in which others fail--are these not talents?--are they not, in the present state of the world, among the most distinguished and influential of mental gifts?

5. And is it not wonderful, that while we should be utterly ashamed to use a superiority of body in order to thrust our weaker companions aside from some place of advantage, we unhesitatingly use our superiorities of mind to thrust them back from whatever good that strength of mind can attain? You would be indignant if you saw a strong man walk into a theatre or lecture-room, and, calmly choosing the best place, take his feeble neighbor by the shoulder, and turn him out of it into the back seats or the street. You would be equally indignant if you saw a stout fellow thrust himself up to a table where some hungry children are being fed, and reach his arm over their heads and take their bread from them.

6. But you are not the least indignant, if, when a man has stoutness of thought and swiftness of capacity, and, instead of being long-armed only, has the much greater gift of being long-headed--you think it perfectly just that he should use his intellect to take the bread out of the mouths of all the other men in the town who are in the same trade with him; or use his breadth and sweep of sight to gather some branch of the commerce of the country into one great cobweb, of which he is himself the central spider, making every thread vibrate with the points of his claws, and commanding every avenue with the facets of his eyes. You see no injustice in this.

7. But there is injustice; and, let us trust, one of which honorable men will at no very distant period disdain to be guilty. In some degree, however, it is indeed not unjust; in some degree it is necessary and intended. It is assuredly just that idleness should be surpassed by energy; that the widest influence should be possessed by those who are best able to wield it; and that a wise man at the end of his career, should be better off than a fool. But for that reason, is the fool to be wretched, utterly crashed down, and left in all the suffering which his conduct and capacity naturally inflict? Not so.

8. What do you suppose fools were made for? That you might tread upon them, and starve them, and get the better of them in every possible way? By no means. They were made that wise people might take care of them. That is the true and plain fact concerning the relations of every strong and wise man to the world about him. He has his strength given him, not that he may crush the weak, but that he may support and guide them. In his own household he is to be the guide and the support of his children; out of his household he is still to be the father, that is, the guide and support, of the weak and the poor; not merely of the meritoriously weak and the innocently poor, but of the guilty and punishably poor; of the men who ought to have known better--of the poor who ought to be ashamed of themselves.

9. It is nothing to give pension and cottage to the widow who has lost her son; it is nothing to give food and medicine to the workman who has broken his arm, or the decrepit woman wasting in sickness. But it is something to use your time and strength in war with the waywardness and thoughtlessness of mankind to keep the erring workman in your service till you have made him an unerring one; and to direct your fellow-merchant to the opportunity which his dullness would have lost.

10. This is much; but it is yet more, when you have fully achieved the superiority which is due to you, and acquired the wealth which is the fitting reward of your sagacity, if you solemnly accept the responsibility of it, as it is the helm and guide of labor far and near. For you who have it in your hands, are in reality the pilots of the power and effort of the State. It is entrusted to you as an authority to be used for good or evil, just as completely as kingly authority was ever given to a prince, or military command to a captain. And according to the quantity of it you have in your hands, you are arbiters of the will and work of the nation; and the whole issue, whether the work of the State shall suffice for the State or not, depends upon you.

11. You may stretch out your sceptre over the heads of the laborers, and say to them, as they stoop to its waving, "Subdue this obstacle that has baffled our fathers; put away this plague that consumes our children; water these dry places, plough these desert ones, carry this food to those who are in hunger; carry this light to those who are in darkness; carry this life to those who are in death;" or on the other side you may say: "Here am I; this power is in my hand; come, build a mound here for me to be throned upon, high and wide; come, make crowns for my head, that men may see them shine from far away; come, weave tapestries for my feet, that I may tread softly on the silk and purple; come, dance before me, that I may slumber; so shall I live in joy, and die in honor." And better than such an honorable death it were, that the day had perished wherein we were born.

12. I trust that in a little while there will be few of our rich men, who, through carelessness or covetousness, thus forfeit the glorious office which is intended for their hands. I said, just now, that wealth ill-used was as the net of the spider, entangling and destroying; but wealth well-used, is as the net of the sacred Fisher who gathers souls of men out of the deep. A time will come--I do not think it is far from us--when this golden net of the world's wealth will be spread abroad as the flaming meshes of morning cloud over the sky; bearing with them the joy of the light and the dew of the morning, as well as the summons to honorable and peaceful toil.

JOHN RUSKIN.

LIFE AND SONG.

[This poem is taken from "The Poems of Sidney Lanier," copyrighted 1891, and published by Charles Scribner's Sons.]

If life were caught by a clarionet,
  And a wild heart, throbbing in the reed,
Should thrill its joy and trill its fret,
  And utter its heart in every deed,

"Then would this breathing clarionet
  Type what the poet fain would be;
For none o' the singers ever yet
  Has wholly lived his minstrelsy,

"Or clearly sung his true, true thought,
  Or utterly bodied forth his life,
Or out of life and song has wrought
  The perfect one of man and wife;

"Or lived and sung, that Life and Song
  Might each express the other's all,
Careless if life or art were long
  Since both were one, to stand or fall:

"So that the wonder struck the crowd,
  Who shouted it about the land:
His song was only living aloud,
  His work, a singing with his hand!"

SIDNEY LANIER.

ELOQUENCE.

1. When public bodies are to be addressed on momentous occasions, when great interests are at stake, and strong passions excited, nothing is valuable in speech farther than as it is connected with high intellectual and moral endowments. Clearness, force, and earnestness are the qualities which produce conviction. True eloquence, indeed, does not consist in speech. It cannot be brought from far. Labor and learning may toil for it, but they will toil in vain. Words and phrases may be marshalled in every way, but they cannot compass it. It must exist in the man, in the subject, and in the occasion.

2. Affected passion, intense expression, the pomp of declamation, all may aspire to it; they cannot reach it. It comes, if it come at all, like the outbreaking of volcanic fires, with spontaneous, original, native force. The graces taught in the schools, the costly ornaments and studied contrivances of speech, shock and disgust men, when their own lives, and the fate of their wives, their children, and their country, hang on the decision of the hour. Then words have lost their power, rhetoric is vain, and all elaborate oratory contemptible. Even genius itself then feels rebuked and subdued, as in the presence of higher qualities.

3. Then patriotism is eloquent; then self-devotion is eloquent. The clear conception, outrunning deductions of logic, the high purpose, the firm resolve, the dauntless spirit, speaking on the tongue, beaming from the eye, informing every feature, and urging the whole man onward, right

onward to his object,--this, this is eloquence; or rather it is something greater and higher than all eloquence,--it is action, noble, sublime, god-like action.

DANIEL WEBSTER.

TRUTH AT LAST.

Does a man ever give up hope, I wonder,--
Face the grim fact, seeing it clear as day?
When Bennen saw the snow slip, heard its thunder
Low, louder, roaring round him, felt the speed
Growing swifter as the avalanche hurled downward,
Did he for just one heart-throb--did he indeed
Know with all certainty, as they swept onward,
There was the end, where the crag dropped away?
Or did he think, even till they plunged and fell,
Some miracle would stop them? Nay, they tell
That he turned round, face forward, calm and pale,
Stretching his arms out toward his native vale.
As if in mute, unspeakable farewell,
And so went down.--'Tis something if at last,
Though only for a flash, a man may see
Clear-eyed the future as he sees the past,
From doubt, or fear, or hope's illusion free.

EDWARD ROWLAND SILL.

WORK.

1. What is wise work, and what is foolish work? What the difference between sense and nonsense, in daily occupation? There are three tests of wise work:--that it must be honest, useful and cheerful.

It is **Honest**. I hardly know anything more strange than that you recognize honesty in play, and do not in work. In your lightest games, you have always some one to see what you call "fair-play." In boxing, you must hit fair; in racing, start fair. Your English watchword is "fair-play," your English hatred, "foul-play." Did it never strike you that you wanted another watchword also, "fair-work," and another and bitterer hatred,--"foul-work"?

2. Then wise work is **Useful**. No man minds, or ought to mind, its being hard, if only it comes to something; but when it is hard and comes to nothing, when all our bees' business turns to spiders', and for honey-comb we have only resultant cobweb, blown away by the next breeze,--that is the cruel thing for the worker. Yet do we ever ask ourselves, personally, or even nationally, whether our work is coming to anything or not?

3. Then wise work is **Cheerful**, as a child's work is. Everybody in this room has been taught to pray daily, "Thy Kingdom come." Now if we hear a man swearing in the streets we think it very wrong, and say he "takes God's name in vain." But there's a twenty times worse way of taking

His name in vain than that. It is to **ask God for what we don't want**. If you don't want a thing don't ask for it: such asking is the worst mockery of your King you can insult Him with. If you do not wish for His kingdom, don't pray for it. But if you do, you must do more than pray for it; you must work for it. And, to work for it, you must know what it is.

4. Observe, it is a Kingdom that is to come to us; we are not to go to it. Also it is not to come all at once, but quietly; nobody knows how. "The Kingdom of God cometh not with observation." Also, it is not to come outside of us, but in our hearts: "The Kingdom of God is within you." Now if we want to work for this Kingdom, and to bring it, and to enter into it, there's one curious condition to be first accepted. We must enter into it as children, or not at all; "Whosoever will not receive it as a little child shall not enter therein." And again, "Suffer little children to come unto me, and forbid them not, **for of such is the Kingdom of Heaven**."

5. Of **such**, observe. Not of children themselves, but of such as children. It is the **character** of children we want and must gain. It is modest, faithful, loving, and because of all these characters it is cheerful. Putting its trust in its father, it is careful for nothing--being full of love to every creature, it is happy always, whether in its play or in its duty. Well, that's the great worker's character also. Taking no thought for the morrow; taking thought only for the duty of the day; knowing indeed what labor is, but not what sorrow is; and always ready for play--beautiful play.

JOHN RUSKIN.

EXTRACT FROM "THE RING AND THE BOOK."

Our human speech is naught,
Our human testimony false, our fame
And human estimation words and wind.
Why take the artistic way to prove so much?
Because, it is the glory and good of Art,
That Art remains the one way possible
Of speaking truth, to mouths like mine, at least.
How look a brother in the face and say
"Thy right is wrong, eyes hast thou, yet art blind,
Thine ears are stuffed and stopped, despite their length,
And, oh, the foolishness thou countest faith!"
Say this as silvery as tongue can troll--
The anger of the man may be endured,
The shrug, the disappointed eyes of him
Are not so bad to bear--but here's the plague,
That all this trouble comes of telling truth,
Which truth, by when it reaches him, looks false,
Seems to be just the thing it would supplant,
Nor recognizable by whom it left;
While falsehood would have done the work of truth.
But Art,--wherein man nowise speaks to men,
Only to mankind,--Art may tell a truth
Obliquely, do the thing shall breed the thought,
Nor wrong the thought, missing the mediate word.

So may you paint your picture, twice show truth,
Beyond mere imagery on the wall,--
So, note by note, bring music from your mind,
Deeper than ever the Adante dived,--
So write a book shall mean, beyond the facts,
Suffice the eye, and save the soul besides.

SELF-RELIANCE.

1. To believe your own thought, to believe that what is true for you in your private heart is true for all men,--that is genius.

Speak your latent conviction, and it shall be the universal sense; for the inmost in due time becomes the outmost, and our first thought is rendered back to us by the trumpets of the Last Judgment. Familiar as the voice of the mind is to each, the highest merit we ascribe to Moses, Plato and Milton is that they all set at naught books and tradition, and spoke not what men but what *they* thought.

2. A man should learn to detect and watch that gleam of light which flashes across his mind from within, more than the lustre of the firmament of bards and sages. Yet he dismisses without notice his thought, because it is his. In every work of genius we recognize our own rejected thoughts; they come back to us with a certain alienated majesty.

3. Great works of art have no more affecting lesson for us than this. They teach us to abide by our spontaneous impression with good-humored inflexibility then most when the whole cry of voices is on the other side. Else to-morrow a stranger will say with masterly good sense precisely what we have thought and felt all the time, and we shall be forced to take with shame our own opinion from another.

4. There is a time in every man's education when he arrives at the conviction that envy is ignorance; that imitation is suicide; that he must take himself for better for worse as his portion; that though the wide universe is full of good, no kernel of nourishing corn can come to him but through his toil bestowed on that plot of ground which is given to him to till. The power which resides in him is new in nature, and none but he knows what that is which he can do, nor does he know until he has tried.

5. Not for nothing one face, one character, one fact makes much impression on him, and another none. This sculpture in the memory is not without preestablished harmony. The eye was placed where one ray should fall, that it might testify of that particular ray.

6. We but half express ourselves, and we are ashamed of that divine idea which each of us represents. It may be safely trusted as proportionate and of good issues, so it be faithfully imparted, but God will not have his work made manifest by cowards. A man is relieved and gay when he has put his heart into his work and done his best; but what he has said or done otherwise shall give him no peace. It is a deliverance which does not deliver. In the attempt his genius deserts him; no muse befriends; no invention, no hope.

7. Trust thyself: every heart vibrates to that iron string. Accept the place the divine providence has found for you, the society of your contemporaries, the connection of events. Great men have always done so, and confided themselves childlike to the genius of their age, betraying their perception that the absolutely trustworthy was seated at their heart, working through their hands, predominating in all their being.

8. And we are now men, and must accept in the highest mind the same transcendent destiny; and not minors and invalids in a protected corner, not cowards fleeing before a revolution, but guides, redeemers and benefactors, obeying the Almighty effort and advancing on Chaos and the

Dark.

RALPH WALDO EMERSON.

RHODORA.

ON BEING ASKED, WHENCE IS THIS FLOWER?

In May, when sea-winds pierced our solitudes,
I found the fresh Rhodora in the woods,
Spreading its leafless blooms in a damp nook,
To please the desert and the sluggish brook.
The purple petals, fallen in the pool,
Made the black water with their beauty gay;
Here might the red-bird come his plumes to cool,
And court the flower that cheapens his array.
Rhodora! if the sages ask thee why
This charm is wasted on the earth and sky,
Tell them, dear, that if eyes were made for seeing,
Then Beauty is its own excuse for being:
Why thou wert there, O rival of the rose!
I never thought to ask, I never knew:
But in my simple ignorance, suppose
The self-same Power that brought me there brought you.

RALPH WALDO EMERSON.

EACH AND ALL.

Little thinks, in the field, yon red-cloaked clown,
Of thee from the hill-top looking down;
The heifer that lows in the upland farm,
Far-heard, lows not thine ear to charm;
The sexton, tolling his bell at noon,
Deems not that great Napoleon
Stops his horse, and lists with delight,
Whilst his files sweep round yon Alpine height;
Nor knowest thou what argument
Thy life to thy neighbor's creed has lent.
All are needed by each one;
Nothing is fair or good alone.

I thought the sparrow's note from heaven,
Singing at dawn on the alder bough;
I brought him home, in his nest, at even;
He sings the song, but it cheers not now,
For I did not bring home the river and sky;--
He sang to my ear,--they sang to my eye.

The delicate shell lay on the shore;
The bubbles of the latest wave
Fresh pearls to their enamel gave,
And the bellowing of the savage sea

Greeted their safe escape to me.
I wiped away the weeds and foam,
I fetched my sea-born treasures home;
But the poor, unsightly, noisome things
Had left their beauty on the shore
With the sun and the sand and the wild uproar.

The lover watched his graceful maid,
As 'mid the virgin train she strayed,
Nor knew her beauty's best attire
Was woven still by the snow-white choir.
At last she came to his hermitage,
Like the bird from the woodlands to the cage;--
The gay enchantment was undone;
A gentle wife, but fairy none.

Then I said, "I covet truth;
Beauty is unripe childhood's cheat;
I leave it behind with the games of youth:"--
As I spoke, beneath my feet
The ground-pine curled its pretty wreath,
Running over the club-moss burrs;
I inhaled the violet's breath;
Around me stood the oaks and firs;
Pine cones and acorns lay on the ground;
Over me soared the eternal sky,
Full of light and of deity;
Again I saw, again I heard,
The rolling river, the morning bird;--
Beauty through my senses stole;
I yielded myself to the perfect whole.

RALPH WALDO EMERSON

COLUMBUS.

[This poem is taken from the complete works of Joaquin Miller, copyrighted, published by the Whitaker Ray Company, San Francisco.]

Behind him lay the gray Azores,
  Behind the gates of Hercules;
Before him not the ghost of shores,
  Before him only shoreless seas.
The good mate said, "Now must we pray,
  For lo! the very stars are gone.
Brave Admiral, speak, what shall I say!"
  "Why, say, 'Sail on! sail on! and on!'"

"My men grow mutinous by day,
  My men grow ghastly pale and weak."
The stout mate thought of home; a spray
  Of salt wave washed his swarthy cheek.
"What shall I say, brave Admiral, say,
  If we sight naught but seas at dawn?"
"Why, you shall say at break of day,
  'Sail on! sail on! sail on! and on!'"

They sailed, and sailed, as winds might blow,
  Until at last the blanched mate said:
"Why, now, not even God would know

Should I and all my men fall dead.
These very winds forget their way,
  For God from these dread seas has gone.
Now speak, brave Admiral, speak and say"--
  He said, "Sail on! sail on! and on!"

They sailed. They sailed. Then spake the mate:
  "This mad sea shows its teeth to-night.
He curls his lips, he lies in wait
  With lifted teeth as if to bite!
Brave Admiral, say but one good word:
  What shall we do when hope is gone?"
The words leapt like a leaping sword,
  "Sail on! sail on! sail on! and on!"

Then, pale and worn, he kept his deck,
  And peered through darkness. Ah, that night
Of all dark nights! And then a speck--
  A light! A light! A light! A light!
It grew, a starlit flag unfurled!
  It grew to be Time's burst of dawn,
He gained a world; he gave that world
  Its grandest lesson: "On! sail on!"

JOAQUIN MILLER.

MY LAST DUCHESS.

FERRARA.

That's my last Duchess painted on the wall,
Looking as if she were alive. I call
That piece a wonder, now; Fra Pandolf's hands
Worked busily a day, and there she stands.
Will't please you sit and look at her? I said.
"Fra Pandolf" by design, for never read
Strangers like you that pictured countenance,
The depth and passion of its earnest glance,
But to myself they turned (since none puts by
The curtain I have drawn for you, but I)
And seemed as they would ask me, if they durst,
How such a glance came there; so, not the first
Are you to turn and ask thus. Sir, 'twas not
Her husband's presence only, called that spot
Of joy into the Duchess' cheek: perhaps
Fra Pandolf chanced to say, "Her mantle laps
Over my Lady's wrist too much," or "Paint
Must never hope to reproduce the faint
Half-flush that dies along her throat;" such stuff
Was courtesy, she thought, and cause enough
For calling up that spot of joy. She had
A heart--how shall I say?--too soon made glad,

Too easily impressed; she liked whate'er
She looked on, and her looks went everywhere
Sir, 'twas all one! My favor at her breast,
The dropping of the daylight in the West,
The bough of cherries some officious fool
Broke in the orchard for her, the white mule
She rode with round the terrace--all and each
Would draw from her alike the approving speech,
Or blush, at least. She thanked men,--good! but thanked
Somehow--I know not how--as if she ranked
My gift of a nine-hundred-years-old name
With anybody's gift. Who'd stoop to blame
This sort of trifling? Even had you skill
In speech--(which I have not)--to make your will
Quite clear to such an one, and say "Just this
"Or that in you disgusts me; here you miss,
"Or there exceed the mark"--and if she let
Herself be lessoned so, nor plainly set
Her wits to yours, forsooth, and made excuse,
--E'en then would be some stooping; and I choose
Never to stoop. Oh, Sir, she smiled, no doubt,
Whene'er I passed her; but who passed without
Much the same smile? This grew; I gave commands;
Then all smiles stopped together. There she stands
As if alive. Will't please you rise? We'll meet
The company below, then. I repeat
The Count your Master's known munificence
Is ample warrant that no just pretence
Of mine for dowry will be disallowed;
Though his fair daughter's self, as I avowed
At starting, is my object. Nay, we'll go
Together down, Sir. Notice Neptune, though,
Taming a sea-horse, thought a rarity,

Which Claus of Innsbruck cast in bronze for me!

ROBERT BROWNING.

"THE TALE."

What a pretty tale you told me
  Once upon a time
--Said you found it somewhere (scold me!)
  Was it prose or rhyme,
Greek or Latin? Greek, you said,
While your shoulder propped my head.

Anyhow there's no forgetting
  This much if no more,
That a poet (pray, no petting!)
  Yes, a bard, sir, famed of yore,
Went where such like used to go,
Singing for a prize, you know.

Well, he had to sing, nor merely
  Sing, but play the lyre;
Playing was important clearly
  Quite as singing; I desire,
Sir, you keep the fact in mind
For a purpose that's behind.

There stood he, while deep attention
  Held the judges round,
--Judges able, I should mention,

To detect the slightest sound
Sung or played amiss: such ears
Had old judges, it appears!

None the less he sang out boldly,
  Played in time and tune
Till the judges, weighing coldly
  Each note's worth, seemed, late or soon,
Sure to smile "In vain one tries
Picking faults out: take the prize!"

When, a mischief! Were they seven
  Strings the lyre possessed?
Oh, and afterwards eleven,
  Thank you! Well, sir--who had guessed
Such ill luck in store?--it happed
One of those same seven strings snapped.

All was lost, then! No! a cricket
  (What "cicada"? Pooh!)
--Some mad thing that left its thicket
  For mere love of music--flew
With its little heart on fire
Lighted on the crippled lyre.

So that when (Ah, joy!) our singer
  For his truant string
Feels with disconcerted finger,
  What does cricket else but fling
Fiery heart forth, sound the note
Wanted by the throbbing throat?

Ay and, ever to the ending,
  Cricket chirps at need,
Executes the hand's intending,
  Promptly, perfectly,--indeed
Saves the singer from defeat
With her chirrup low and sweet.

Till, at ending, all the judges
  Cry with one assent
"Take the prize--a prize who grudges
  Such a voice and instrument?
Why, we took your lyre for harp,
So it shrilled us forth F sharp!"

Did the conqueror spurn the creature,
  Once its service done?
That's no such uncommon feature
  In the case when Music's son
Finds his Lotte's power too spent
For aiding soul development.

No! This other, on returning
  Homeward, prize in hand,
Satisfied his bosom's yearning:
  (Sir! I hope you understand!)
--Said "Some record there must be
Of this cricket's help to me!"

So he made himself a statue:
  Marble stood, life-size;
On the lyre, he pointed at you,
  Perched his partner in the prize;
Never more apart you found

Her, he throned, from him, she crowned.

That's the tale: its application?
  Somebody I know
Hopes one day for reputation
  Through his poetry that's--Oh,
All so learned and so wise
And deserving of a prize!

If he gains one, will some ticket,
  When his statue's built,
Tell the gazer "'Twas a cricket
  Helped my crippled lyre, whose lilt
Sweet and low, when strength usurped
Softness' place i' the scale, she chirped?

"For as victory was nighest,
  While I sang and played,--
With my lyre at lowest, highest,
  Right alike,--one string that made
'Love' sound soft was snapt in twain
Never to be heard again,--

"Had not a kind cricket fluttered,
  Perched upon the place
Vacant left, and duly uttered
  'Love, Love, Love,' whene'er the bass
Asked the treble to atone
For its somewhat sombre drone."

But you don't know music! Wherefore
  Keep on casting pearls
To a--poet? All I care for

Is--to tell him a girl's
"Love" comes aptly in when gruff
Grows his singing. (There, enough!)

ROBERT BROWNING.

MONT BLANC BEFORE SUNRISE.

Hast thou a charm to stay the morning-star
In his steep course? So long he seems to pause
On thy bald, awful head, O sovereign Blanc!
The Arve and Arveiron at thy base
Rave ceaselessly; but thou, most awful form,
Risest from forth thy silent sea of pines,
How silently! Around thee, and above,
Deep is the air and dark, substantial, black,
An ebon mass: methinks thou piercest it
As with a wedge. But when I look again
It is thine own calm home, thy crystal shrine,
Thy habitation from eternity.

O dread and silent Mount! I gazed upon thee
Till thou, still present to the bodily sense,
Didst vanish from my thought: entranced in prayer
I worshipped the Invisible alone.
Yet, like some sweet beguiling melody,--
So sweet we know not we are listening to it,--
Thou, the mean while wast blending with my thought.
Yea, with my life, and life's own secret joy;
Till the dilating soul, enrapt, transfused,
Into the mighty vision passing--there,
As in her natural form, swelled vast to heaven.

Awake, my soul! not only passive praise
Thou owest! not alone these swelling tears,
Mute thanks, and secret ecstasy! Awake,
Voice of sweet song! Awake, my heart, awake!
Green vales and icy cliffs! all join my hymn!

Thou first and chief, sole sovereign of the vale!
O, struggling with the darkness all the night,
And visited all night by troops of stars,
Or when they climb the sky, or when they sink,--
Companion of the morning-star at dawn,
Thyself earth's rosy star, and of the dawn
Co-herald--wake! O wake! and utter praise!
Who sank thy sunless pillars deep in earth?
Who filled thy countenance with rosy light?
Who made thee parent of perpetual streams?

And you, ye five wild torrents fiercely glad!
Who called you forth from night and utter death,
From dark and icy caverns called you forth,
Down those precipitous, black, jagged rocks,
Forever shattered, and the same forever?
Who gave you your invulnerable life,
Your strength, your speed, your fury and your joy,
Unceasing thunder, and eternal foam?
And who commanded,--and the silence came,--
"Here let the billows stiffen and have rest?"

Ye ice-falls! ye that from the mountain's brow
Adown enormous ravines slope amain--
Torrents, methinks, that heard a mighty voice,
And stopped at once amid their maddest plunge!
Motionless torrents! silent cataracts!

Who made you glorious as the gates of heaven
Beneath the keen full moon? Who bade the sun
Clothe you with rainbows? Who, with living flowers
Of loveliest blue, spread garlands at your feet?

"God!" let the torrents, like a shout of nations,
Answer! and let the ice-plain echo, "God!"
"God!" sing, ye meadow streams, with gladsome voice
Ye pine groves, with your soft and soul-like sounds
And they, too, have a voice, yon piles of snow,
And in their perilous fall shall thunder, "God!"

Ye living flowers that skirt the eternal frost!
Ye wild goats sporting round the eagle's nest!
Ye eagles, playmates of the mountain storm!
Ye lightnings, the dread arrows of the clouds!
Ye signs and wonders of the elements!
Utter forth "God!" and fill the hills with praise!

Thou too, hoar mount! with thy sky-pointing peaks
Oft from whose feet the avalanche, unheard
Shoots downward, glittering through the pure serene
Into the depth of clouds that veil thy breast,--
Thou too, again, stupendous mountain! thou
That, as I raise my head, awhile bowed low
In adoration, upward from thy base
Slow traveling, with dim eyes suffused with tears,
Solemnly seemest, like a vapory cloud
To rise before me,--rise, oh, ever rise!
Rise, like a cloud of incense, from the earth!
Thou kingly spirit, throned among the hills,
Thou dread ambassador from earth to heaven,
Great Hierarch! tell thou the silent sky,

And tell the stars, and tell yon rising sun,
Earth, with her thousand voices, praises God.

S.T. COLERIDGE.

MY STAR.

All that I know
  Of a certain star
Is, it can throw
  (Like the angled spar)
Now a dart of red,
  Now a dart of blue,
Till my friends have said
  They would fain see, too

My star that dartles the red and the blue!
Then it stops like a bird; like a flower, hangs furled;
They must solace themselves with the Saturn above it.
What matter to me if their star is a world?
Mine has opened its soul to me; therefore I love it.

ROBERT BROWNING.

A CONSERVATIVE.

The garden beds I wandered by
  One bright and cheerful morn,
When I found a new-fledged butterfly
  A-sitting on a thorn,
A black and crimson butterfly,
  All doleful and forlorn.

I thought that life could have no sting
  To infant butterflies,
So I gazed on this unhappy thing
  With wonder and surprise,
While sadly with his waving wing
  He wiped his weeping eyes.

Said I, "What can the matter be?
  Why weepest thou so sore?
With garden fair and sunlight free
  And flowers in goodly store--"
But he only turned away from me
  And burst into a roar.

Cried he, "My legs are thin and few
  Where once I had a swarm!
Soft fuzzy fur--a joy to view--

Once kept my body warm,
Before these flapping wing-things grew,
  To hamper and deform!"

At that outrageous bug I shot
  The fury of mine eye;
Said I, in scorn all burning hot,
  In rage and anger high,
"You ignominious idiot!
  Those wings are made to fly!"

"I do not want to fly," said he,
  "I only want to squirm!"
And he drooped his wings dejectedly,
  But still his voice was firm;
"I do not want to be a fly!
  I want to be a worm!"

O yesterday of unknown lack!
  To-day of unknown bliss!
I left my fool in red and black,
  The last I saw was this,--
The creature madly climbing back
  Into his chrysalis.

CHARLOTTE PERKINS GILMAN.

FIVE LIVES.

Five mites of monads dwelt in a round drop
That twinkled on a leaf by a pool in the sun.
To the naked eye they lived invisible;
Specks, for a world of whom the empty shell
Of a mustard-seed had been a hollow sky.

One was a meditative monad, called a sage;
And, shrinking all his mind within, he thought:
"Tradition, handed down for hours and hours,
Tells that our globe, this quivering crystal world,
Is slowly dying. What if, seconds hence,
When I am very old, yon shimmering dome
Come drawing down and down, till all things end?"
Then with a weazen smirk he proudly felt
No other mote of God had ever gained
Such giant grasp of universal truth.

One was a transcendental monad; thin
And long and slim in the mind; and thus he mused:
"Oh, vast, unfathomable monad-Souls!
Made in the image"--a hoarse frog croaks from the pool--
"Hark! 'twas some god, voicing his glorious thought
In thunder music! Yea, we hear their voice,
And we may guess their minds from ours, their work.

Some taste they have like ours, some tendency
To wiggle about, and munch a trace of scum."
He floated up on a pin-point bubble of gas
That burst, pricked by the air, and he was gone.

One was a barren-minded monad, called
A positivist; and he knew positively:
"There is no world beyond this certain drop.
Prove me another! Let the dreamers dream
Of their faint gleams, and noises from without,
And higher and lower; life is life enough."
Then swaggering half a hair's breadth, hungrily
He seized upon an atom of bug and fed.

One was a tattered monad, called a poet;
And with shrill voice ecstatic thus he sang:
"Oh, the little female monad's lips!
Oh, the little female monad's eyes!
Ah, the little, little, female, female monad!"

The last was a strong-minded monadess,
Who dashed amid the infusoria,
Danced high and low, and wildly spun and dove
Till the dizzy others held their breath to see.

But while they led their wondrous little lives
AEonian moments had gone wheeling by.
The burning drop had shrunk with fearful speed;
A glistening film--'twas gone; the leaf was dry.
The little ghost of an inaudible squeak
Was lost to the frog that goggled from his stone;
Who, at the huge, slow tread of a thoughtful ox
Coming to drink, stirred sideways fatly, plunged,

Launched backward twice, and all the pool was still.

EDWARD ROWLAND SILL.

THE COMING OF ARTHUR.

[Abridged.]

LEODOGRAN, the King of Cameliard,
Had one fair daughter, and none other child;
And she was fairest of all flesh on earth,
Guinevere, and in her his one delight.

  For many a petty king ere Arthur came
Ruled in this isle and, ever waging war
Each upon other, wasted all the land;
And still from time to time the heathen host
Swarm'd over seas, and harried what was left.
And so there grew great tracts of wilderness,
Wherein the beast was ever more and more,
But man was less and less. . . .

  And thus the land of Cameliard was waste,
Thick with wet woods, and many a beast therein,
And none or few to scare or chase the beast;
So that wild dog and wolf and boar and bear
Came night and day, and rooted in the fields,
And wallow'd in the gardens of the King.

    . . . . .   And King Leodogran

Groan'd for the Roman legions here again
And Caesar's eagle. .   .   .   .

He knew not whither he should turn for aid.

But--for he heard of Arthur newly crown'd,
. . . .--the King
Sent to him, saying, 'Arise and help us thou!
For here between the man and beast we die.'

And Arthur yet had done no deed of arms,
But heard the call and came; and Guinevere
Stood by the castle walls to watch him pass;
But since he neither wore on helm or shield
The golden symbol of his kinglihood,
But rode, a simple knight among his knights,
And many of these in richer arms than he,
She saw him not, or marked not, if she saw,
One among many, tho' his face was bare.
But Arthur, looking downward as he past,
Felt the light of her eyes into his life
Smite on the sudden, yet rode on, and pitch'd
His tents beside the forest. Then he drave
The heathen; after, slew the beast, and fell'd
The forest, letting in the sun, and made
Broad pathways for the hunter and the knight
And so returned.

For while he linger'd there,
A doubt that ever smoulder'd in the hearts
Of those great lords and barons of his realm
Flashed forth and into war; for most of these,
Colleaguing with a score of petty kings,

Made head against him crying: "Who is he
That should rule us? Who hath proven him
King Uther's son?"

And, Arthur, passing thence to battle, felt
Travail, and throes and agonies of the life,
Desiring to be join'd with Guinevere,
And thinking as he rode: "Her father said
That there between the man and beast they die.
Shall I not lift her from this land of beasts
Up to my throne and side by side with me?
What happiness to reign a lonely king?

. . . . But were I join'd with her,
Then might we live together as one life,
And reigning with one will in everything
Have power on this dark land to lighten it,
And power on this dead world to make it live."

When Arthur reached a field of battle bright
With pitch'd pavilions of his foe, the world
Was all so clear about him that he saw
The smallest rock far on the faintest hill,
And even in high day the morning star.

. . . . But the Powers who walk the world,
Made lightnings and great thunders over him,
And dazed all eyes, till Arthur by main might,
And mightier of his hands with every blow,
And leading all his knighthood, threw the kings.

So like a painted battle the war stood
Silenced, the living quiet as the dead,

And in the heart of Arthur joy was lord.

Then quickly from the foughten field he sent
. . . . Sir Bedivere
. . . . to King Leodogran,
Saying, "If I in aught have served thee well,
Give me thy daughter Guinevere to wife."

Whom when he heard, Leodogran in heart
Debating--"How should I that am a king,
However much he holp me at my need,
Give my one daughter saving to a king,
And a king's son"?--lifted his voice, and call'd
A hoary man, his chamberlain, to whom
He trusted all things, and of him required
His counsel: "Knowest thou aught of Arthur's birth?"

Then while the King debated with himself,

. . . . . there came to Cameliard,

Lot's wife, the Queen of Orkney, Bellicent;
Whom . . . . the King
Made feast for, as they sat at meat:

'Ye come from Arthur's court.   Victor his men
Report him! Yea, but ye--think ye this king--
So many those that hate him, and so strong,
So few his knights, however brave they be--
Hath body enow to hold his foeman down?'

'O King,' she cried, 'and I will tell thee: few,
Few, but all brave, all of one mind with him;

For I was near him when the savage yells
Of Uther's peerage died, and Arthur sat
Crowned on the dais, and all his warriors cried,
"Be thou the King, and we will work thy will
Who love thee,"   Then the King in low deep tones,
And simple words of great authority,
Bound them by so straight vows to his own self
That when they rose, knighted from kneeling, some
Were pale as at the passing of a ghost,
Some flush'd, and others dazed, as one who wakes
Half blinded at the coming of a light.

'But when he spake, and cheer'd his Table Round
With large, divine, and comfortable words,
Beyond my tongue to tell thee--I beheld
From eye to eye thro' all their Order flash
A momentary likeness of the King;

 'And there I saw mage Merlin, whose vast wit
And hundred winters are but as the hands
Of loyal vassals toiling for their liege.

  'And near him stood the Lady of the Lake,
Who knew a subtler magic than his own--
Clothed in white samite, mystic, wonderful.
She gave the King his huge cross-hilted sword,
Whereby to drive the heathen out: a mist
Of incense curl'd about her, and her face
Wellnigh was hidden in the minster gloom;
But there was heard among the holy hymns
A voice as of the waters, for she dwells
Down in a deep--calm, whatsoever storms
May shake the world--and when the surface rolls,

Hath power to walk the waters like our Lord.'

   Thereat Leodogran rejoiced, but thought
To sift his doubtings to the last, and ask'd,
Fixing full eyes of question on her face,
'The swallow and the swift are near akin,
But thou art closer to this noble prince,
Being his own dear sister;'

    . . . . 'What know I?
For dark my mother was in eyes and hair,
And dark in hair and eyes am I; . .
   . . . . yea and dark was Uther too,
Wellnigh to blackness; but this king is fair
Beyond the race of Britons and of men.

   'But let me tell thee now another tale:

    . . . . on the night
When Uther in Tintagil past away
Moaning and wailing for an heir, Merlin
Left the still King, and passing forth to breathe,

Beheld, so high upon the dreary deeps
It seem'd in heaven, a ship, the shape thereof
A dragon wing'd and all from stem to stern
Bright with a shining people on the decks,
And gone as soon as seen. . . . . . He
    . . . . . watch'd the great sea fall,
Wave after wave, each mightier than the last,
Till last, a ninth one, gathering half the deep
And full of voices, slowly rose and plunged
Roaring, and all the wave was in a flame:

And down the wave and in the flame was borne
A naked babe, and rode to Merlin's feet,
Who stoopt and caught the babe, and cried, "The King!"

And presently thereafter follow'd calm,
Free sky and stars: "And this same child," he said,
"Is he who reigns." . . . .

. . . . . . And ever since the Lords
Have foughten like wild beasts among themselves,
So that the realm has gone to wrack; but now,
This year, when Merlin--for his hour had come--
Brought Arthur forth, and sat him in the hall,
Proclaiming, "Here is Uther's heir, your King,"
A hundred voices cried: "Away with him!
No king of ours!" . . . . .

. . . . Yet Merlin thro' his craft,
And while the people clamor'd for a king,
Had Arthur crown'd; but after, the great lords
Banded, and so brake out in open war.

. . . . and Merlin in our time
Hath spoken also, ...
Tho' men may wound him that he will not die,
But pass, again to come, and then or now
Utterly smite the heathen under foot,
Till these and all men hail him for their king.'

. . . . . King Leodogran rejoiced,
But musing 'Shall I answer yea or nay?'
Doubted, and drowsed, nodded and slept, and saw,
Dreaming a slope of land that ever grew,

Field after field, up to a height, the peak
Haze-hidden, and thereon a phantom king,
Now looming, and now lost; and on the slope
The sword rose, the hind fell, the herd was driven,
Fire glimpsed; and all the land from roof and rick,
In drifts of smoke before a rolling wind,
Stream'd to the peak, and mingled with the haze
And made it thicker; while the phantom king
Sent out at times a voice; and here or there
Stood one who pointed toward the voice, the rest
Slew on and burnt, crying, 'No king of ours,
No son of Uther, and no king of ours;'
Till with a wink his dream was changed, the haze
Descended, and the solid earth became
As nothing, but the king stood out in heaven,
Crown'd. And Leodogran awoke, and sent

Back to the court of Arthur answering yea.

  Then Arthur charged his warrior whom he loved
And honor'd most, Sir Lancelot, to ride forth
And bring the Queen, and watched him from the gates:
And Lancelot past away among the flowers--
For then was latter April--and return'd--
Among the flowers, in May, with Guinevere.
To whom arrived, by Dubric the high saint,
Chief of the church in Britain, and before
The stateliest of her altar-shrines, the King
That morn was married, while in stainless white,
The fair beginners of a noble time,
And glorying in their vows and him, his knights
Stood around him, and rejoicing in his joy.
Far shone the fields of May thro' open door,

The sacred altar blossom'd white with May,
The sun of May descended on their King,
They gazed on all earth's beauty in their Queen,
Roll'd incense, and there past along the hymns
A voice as of the waters, while the two
Sware at the shrine of Christ a deathless love.
And Arthur said, 'Behold, thy doom is mine.
Let chance what will, I love thee to the death!'
To whom the Queen replied with drooping eyes,
'King and my Lord, I love thee to the death!'
And holy Dubric spread his hands and spake:
'Reign ye, and live and love, and make the world
Other, and may the Queen be one with thee,
And all this Order of thy Table Round
Fulfil the boundless purpose of their King!'

And Arthur's knighthood sang before the King:--

  'Blow trumpet, for the world is white with May!!
Blow trumpet, the long night hath roll'd away!
Blow thro' the living world--"Let the King reign!"

  'Shall Rome or Heathen rule in Arthur's realm?
Flash brand and lance, fall battle-axe on helm,
Fall battle-axe, and flash brand! Let the King reign!

  'Strike for the King and live! his knights have heard
That God hath told the King a secret word.
Fall battle-axe and flash brand! Let the King reign!

  'Strike for the King and die! and if thou diest,
The king is king, and ever wills the highest.
Clang battle-axe, and clash brand! Let the King reign!

'The King will follow Christ, and we the King,
In whom high God hath breathed a secret thing.
Fall battle-axe, and clash brand! "Let the King reign!"

And Arthur and his knighthood for a space
Were all one will, and thro' that strength the King
Drew in the petty princedoms under him,
Fought, and in twelve great battles overcame
The heathen hordes, and made a realm and reign'd.

ALFRED, LORD TENNYSON.

ELAINE.

Elaine the fair, Elaine the lovable,
Elaine, the lily maid of Astolat,
High in her chamber up a tower to the east
Guarded the sacred shield of Lancelot;
Which first she placed where morning's earliest ray
Might strike it, and awaken her with the gleam;
Then fearing rust or soilure, fashion'd for it
A case of silk, and braided thereupon
All the devices blazon'd on the shield
In their own tinct, and added, of her wit,
A border fantasy of branch and flower,
And yellow-throated nestling in the nest.
Nor rested thus content, but day by day
Leaving her household and good father, climb'd
That eastern tower, and entering barr'd the door,
Stript off the case, and read the naked shield,
Now guess'd a hidden meaning in his arms,
Now made a pretty history to herself
Of every dint a sword had beaten in it,
And every scratch a lance had made upon it,
Conjecturing when and where: this cut is fresh;
That ten years back; this dealt him at Caerlyle;
That at Cearleon; this at Camelot;
And ah, God's mercy what a stroke was there!

And here a thrust that might have kill'd, but God
Broke the Strong lance and roll'd his enemy down,
And saved him; so she lived in fantasy.

ALFRED, LORD TENNYSON

THE LADY OF SHALOTT.

PART I.

On either side the river lie
Long fields of barley and of rye,
That clothe the wold and meet the sky;
And thro' the field the road runs by
  To many-tower'd Camelot
And up and down the people go,
Gazing where the lilies blow
Round an island there below,
    The Island of Shalott.

Willows whiten, aspens quiver,
Little breezes, dusk and shiver
Thro' the wave that runs for ever
By the island in the river
    Flowing down to Camelot.
Four gray walls, and four gray towers,
Overlook a space of flowers,
And the silent isle imbowers
    The lady of Shalott.

By the margin, willow-veil'd,
Slide the heavy barges trail'd

By slow horses; and unhail'd
The shallop flitteth silken-sail'd
   Skimming down to Camelot:
But who hath seen her wave her hand?
Or at the casement seen her stand?
Or is she known in all the land,
    The Lady of Shalott?

Only reapers, reaping early
In among the bearded barley,
Hear a song that echoes cheerly,
From the river winding clearly,
   Down to tower'd Camelot;
And by the moon the reaper weary,
Piling sheaves in uplands airy,
Listening, whispers "'Tis the fairy
  Lady of Shalott."

PART II.

There she weaves by night and day
A magic web with colors gay.
She has heard a whisper say,
A curse is on her if she stay
  To look down to Camelot.
She knows not what the curse may be,
And so she weaveth steadily,
And little other care hath she,
  The Lady of Shalott.

And moving thro' a mirror clear
That hangs before her all the year,

Shadows of the world appear.
There she sees the highway near
  Winding down to Camelot;
There the river eddy whirls,
And there the surly village-churls,
And the red cloaks of market-girls,
  Pass onward from Shalott.

Sometimes a troop of damsels glad,
An abbot on an ambling pad,
Sometimes a curly shepherd-lad,
Or long-hair'd page in crimson clad,
  Goes by to tower'd Camelot;
And sometimes thro' the mirror blue
The knights come riding two and two;
She hath no loyal knight and true,
  The Lady of Shalott.

But in her web she still delights
To weave the mirror's magic sights,
For often thro' the silent nights
A funeral, with plumes and lights,
  And music, went to Camelot:
Or when the moon was overhead,
Came two young lovers lately wed:
"I am half sick of shadows" said
  The Lady of Shalott.

PART III.

A bow-shot from her bower-eaves,
He rode between the barley sheaves,
The sun came dazzling thro' the leaves,
And flamed upon the brazen greaves
  Of bold Sir Lancelot.
A red-cross knight for ever kneel'd
To a lady in his shield,
That sparkled on the yellow field,
  Beside remote Shalott.

The gemmy bridle glitter'd free,
Like to some branch of stars we see
Hung in the Golden Galaxy.
The bridle bells rang merrily
  As he rode down to Camelot;
And from his blazon'd baldric slung
A mighty silver bugle hung,
And as he rode his armor rung,
    Beside remote Shalott.

All in the blue unclouded weather
Thick-jewell'd shone the saddle-leather.
The helmet and the helmet-feather
Burned like one burning flame together,
    As he rode down to Camelot;
As often through the purple night,
Below the starry clusters bright,
Some bearded meteor, trailing light,
    Moves over still Shalott.

His broad clear brow in sunlight glow'd;
On burnish'd hooves his war-horse trode;
From underneath his helmet flow'd
His coal-black curls as on he rode,
    As he rode down to Camelot.
From the bank and from the river
He flashed into the crystal mirror,
"Tirra lirra" by the river
    Sang Sir Lancelot.

She left the web, she left the loom,
She made three paces thro' the room,
She saw the water-lily bloom,
She saw the helmet and the plume,
    She looked down to Camelot.
Out flew the web and floated wide;
The mirror cracked from side to side;
"The curse is come upon me," cried
    The Lady of Shalott.

PART IV.

In the stormy east-wind straining,
The pale yellow woods are waning,
The broad stream in his banks complaining,
Heavily the low sky raining
    Over tower'd Camelot;
Down she came and found a boat
Beneath a willow left afloat,
And round about the prow she wrote
    The Lady of Shalott.

And down the river's dim expanse
Like some bold seer in a trance,
Seeing all his own mischance--
With a glassy countenance
  Did she look to Camelot.
And at the closing of the day
She loosed the chain, and down she lay;
The broad stream bore her far away,
  The Lady of Shalott.

Lying, robed in snowy white
That loosely flew to left and right--
The leaves upon her falling light--
Thro' the noises of the night
  She floated down to Camelot;
And as the boat-head wound along
The willowy hills and fields among,
They heard her singing her last song,
  The Lady of Shalott.

Heard a carol, mournful, holy,
Chanted loudly, chanted lowly,
Til' her blood was frozen slowly,
And her eyes were darken'd wholly,
  Turn'd to tower'd Camelot.
For ere she reached upon the tide
The first house by the water-side,
Singing in her song she died.
  The Lady of Shalott.

Under tower and balcony,
By garden-wall and gallery,
A gleaming shape she floated by,

Dead-pale between the houses high,
  Silent into Camelot.
Out upon the wharfs they came,
Knight and burgher, lord and dame,
And round the prow they read her name
  The Lady of Shalott.

Who is this? and what is here?
And in the lighted palace near
Died the sound of royal cheer;
And they crossed themselves for fear,
  All the knights at Camelot:
But Lancelot mused a little space;
He said "She has a lovely face;
God in his mercy lend her grace,
    The Lady of Shalott."

ALFRED, LORD TENNYSON.

IF WE HAD THE TIME.

If I had the time to find a place
And sit me down full face to face
  With my better self, that cannot show
  In my daily life that rushes so:
It might be then I would see my soul
Was stumbling still towards the shining goal,
  I might be nerved by the thought sublime,--
    If I had the time!

If I had the time to let my heart
Speak out and take in my life a part,
  To look about and to stretch a hand
  To a comrade quartered in no-luck land;
Ah, God! If I might but just sit still
And hear the note of the whip-poor-will,
  I think that my wish with God's would rhyme--
    If I had the time!

If I had the time to learn from you
How much for comfort my word could do;
  And I told you then of my sudden will
  To kiss your feet when I did you ill;
If the tears aback of the coldness feigned
Could flow, and the wrong be quite explained,--

Brothers, the souls of us all would chime,
  If we had the time!

RICHARD BURTON.

A SCENE FROM KING HENRY IV.
"FALSTAFF'S RECRUITS."

Introduction.--Sir John Falstaff has received a commission from the
King to raise a company of soldiers to fight in the King's battles. After
drafting a number of well-to-do farmers, whom he knows will pay him snug
sums of money rather than to serve under him, he pockets their money and
proceeds to fill his company from the riff-raff of the country through
which he passes.

The scene is a village green before Justice Shallow's house. The Justice
has received word from Sir John that he is about to visit him, and desires
him to call together a number of the villagers from which recruits may be
selected.

These villagers are now grouped upon the green, with Justice Shallow
standing near.

Bardolph, Sir John Falstaff's corporal, enters and addresses Justice
Shallow.

Bardolph.--Good morrow, honest gentlemen. I beseech you, which is
Justice Shallow?

Shallow.--I am Robert Shallow, sir; a poor esquire of this county,
and one of the King's justices of the peace. What is your good pleasure

with me?

Bardolph.--My captain, sir, commends him to you; my captain, Sir
John Falstaff, a tall gentlemen, by heaven, and a most gallant leader.

Shallow.--He greets me well, sir. I knew him a good backsword man.
How doth the good Knight now? Look! here comes good Sir John. (Enter
Falstaff.) Give me your good hand, give me your worship's good hand.
By my troth you look well and bear your years very well; welcome, good Sir
John.

Falstaff.--I am glad to see you well, good Master Robert Shallow.
Fie, this is hot weather, gentlemen. Have you provided me with half a
dozen sufficient men?

Shallow.--Marry have we, sir.

Falstaff.--Let me see them, I beseech you.

Shallow.--Where's the roll? Where's the roll? Where's the roll? Let
me see, let me see, let me see. So, so, so, so, so, so, so; yea, marry
sir.--Ralph Mouldy! Let them appear as I call; let them do so, let them do
so. Let me see; where is Mouldy?

Mouldy.--Here, an't please you.

Shallow.--What think you, Sir John? A good limbed fellow: young,
strong, and of good friends.

Falstaff.--Is thy name Mouldy?

Mouldy.--Yea, an't please you.

Falstaff.--'Tis the more time thou wert used.

Shallow.--Ha, ha, ha! most excellent, i' faith! Things that are
mouldy lack use; very singular good! Well said, Sir John, very well said.
Shall I prick him, Sir John?

Falstaff.--Yes, prick him.

Mouldy.--I was pricked well enough before, an' you could have let
me alone; my old dame will be undone now for one to do her husbandry and
her drudgery; you need not to have pricked me; there are other men fitter
to go out than I.

Shallow.--Peace, fellow, peace! Stand aside; know you where you
are? For the next, Sir John; let me see.--Simon Shadow?

Falstaff.--Yea, marry, let me have him to sit under. He's like to
be a cold soldier.

Shallow.--Where's Shadow?

Shadow.--Here, sir.

Falstaff.--Shadow, whose son art thou?

Shadow.--My mother's son, sir.

Falstaff.--Thy mother's son! Like enough, and thy father's shadow.
Prick him. Shadow will serve for summer.

Shallow.--Thomas Wart!

Falstaff.--Where's he?

Wart.--Here, sir!

Falstaff.--Is thy name Wart?

Wart.--Yea, sir.

Falstaff.--Thou art a very ragged wart.

Shallow.--Ha, ha, ha! Shall I prick him down, Sir John?

Falstaff.--It were superfluous; for his apparel is built upon his
back and the whole frame stands upon pins; prick him no more.

Shallow.--Ha, ha, ha! you can do it, sir; you can do it; I commend
you well.--Francis Feeble.

Feeble.--Here, sir.

Falstaff.--What trade art thou, Feeble?

Feeble.--I'm a woman's tailor, sir.

Falstaff.--Well, good woman's tailor, wilt thou make as many holes
in an enemy's battle as thou hast done in a woman's petticoat?

Feeble.--I will do my good will, sir; you can have no more.

Falstaff.--Well said, good woman's tailor! Well said, courageous
Feeble! Thou wilt be as valiant as the wrathful dove, or most magnanimous
mouse. Prick me the woman's tailor well, Master Shallow; deep, Master

Shallow.

Feeble.--I would Wart might have gone, too, sir.

Falstaff.--I would thou wert a man's tailor, that thou mightst mend him and make him fit to go. Let that suffice, most forcible Feeble.

Feeble.--It shall suffice, sir.

Falstaff.--I am bound to thee, reverend Feeble. Who is next?

Shallow.--Peter Bullcalf, o' the green.

Falstaff.--Yea, marry, let's see Bullcalf.

Bullcalf.--Here, sir.

Falstaff.--Fore God, a likely fellow! Come, prick me Bullcalf till he roar again.

Bullcalf.--O Lord! Good my lord captain,--

Falstaff.--What, dost thou roar before thou art pricked?

Bullcalf.--O Lord, sir! I'm a diseased man.

Falstaff.--What disease hast thou?

Bullcalf.--A terrible cold, sir, a cough, sir.

Falstaff.--Come, thou shalt go to the wars in a gown. We will have away with thy cold. Is here all?

Shallow.--Here is two more than your number. You must have but four here, sir; and so, I pray you, go in with me to dinner.

Falstaff.--Come, I will go drink with you.

(Exit Sir John and Justice Shallow.)

Bullcalf.--(Approaching Bardolph.) Good Master Corporate Bardolph, stand my friend; and here's four Harry ten shillings in French crowns for you. In very truth, sir, I'd as lief be hanged, sir, as to go; and yet for mine own part, sir, I do not care; but rather because I am unwilling, and, for mine own part, have a desire to stay with my friends; else, sir, I did not care, for my own part, so much.

Bardolph.--(Pocketing the money.) Go to; stand aside.

Feeble.--By my troth, I care not.

WILLIAM SHAKESPEARE.

A SCENE FROM DAVID COPPERFIELD.

AT THE LODGINGS OF MR. AND MRS. MICAWBER.

Introduction.--The scene opens in the lodgings of Mr. and Mrs. Micawber. Mr. Micawber at this time is suffering under, what he terms, "A temporary pressure of pecuniary liabilities," and is out looking for something to turn up.

Mrs. Micawber is at home attending to the twins, one of which she is holding in her arms, the other is in the cradle near by, and various of the children are scattered about the floor.

Mrs. Micawber has been bothered all the morning by the calling of creditors;--at last she exclaims, as she trots the babe in her arms:--

(Mrs. Micawber.) Well, I wonder how many more times they will be calling! However, it's their fault. If Mr. Micawber's creditors won't give him time, they must take the consequences. Oh! there is some one knocking now! I believe that's Mr. Heep's knock. It *is* Mr. Heep! Come in, Mr. Heep. We are very glad to see you. Come right in.

Heep.--Is Mr. Micawber in?

Mrs. Mic.--No, Mr. Heep. Mr. Micawber has gone out. We make no stranger of you, Mr. Heep, so I don't mind telling you Mr. Micawber's affairs have reached a crisis. With the exception of a heel of Dutch cheese, which is not adapted to the wants of a young family,--and including the twins,--there is nothing to eat in the house.

Heep.--How dreadful! (Aside.) The very man for my purpose. (Explanation. At this moment there is a noise heard on the landing. Micawber himself rushes into the room, slamming the door behind him.)

Micawber.--(Not seeing Heep.) The clouds have gathered, the storm has broken, and the thunderbolt has fallen on the devoted head of Wilkins Micawber! Emma, my dear, the die is cast. All is over. Leave me in my misery!

Mrs. Mic.--I'll never desert my Micawber!

Mic.--In the words of the immortal Plato, "It must be so, Cato!" But no man is without a friend when he is possessed of courage and shaving materials! Emma, my love, fetch me my razors! (Recovers himself) sh--sh! We are not alone! (Gayly) Oh, Mr. Heep! Delighted to see you, my young friend! Ah, my dear young attorney-general, in prospective, if I had only known you when my troubles commenced, my creditors would have been a great deal better managed than they were! You will pardon the momentary laceration of a wounded spirit, made sensitive by a recent collision with a minion of the law,--in short, with a ribald turncock attached to the waterworks. Emma, my love, our supply of water has been cut off. Hope has sunk beneath the horizon! Bring me a pint of laudanum!

Heep.--Mr. Micawber, would you be willing to tell me the amount of your indebtedness?

Mic.--It is only a small matter for nutriment, beef, mutton, etc., some trifle, seven and six pence ha'penny.

Heep.--I'll pay it for you.

Mic.--My dear friend! You overpower me with obligation! Shall I admit the officer? (Turns and goes to the door, opens it.) Enter myrmidon! Hats off, in the presence of a solvent debtor and a lady. (Heeps pays the officer and dismisses him.)

Heep.--Now, Mr. Micawber, I suppose you have no objection to giving me your I.O.U. for the amount.

Mic.--Certainly not. I am always ready to put my name to any species of negotiable paper, from twenty shillings upward. Excuse me, Heep, I'll write it. (Goes through motion of writing it on leaf of memo, book. Tears it out and hands it to Heep.) I suppose this is renewable on the usual term?

Heep.--Better. You can work it out. I come to offer you the position of clerk in my partner's office--the firm of Wickfield and Heep.

Mic.--What! A clerk! Emma, my love, I believe I may have no hesitation in saying something has at last turned up!

Heep.--You will excuse me, Mrs. Micawber, but I should like to speak a few words to your husband in private.

Mrs. Mic.--Certainly! Wilkins, my love, go on and prosper!

Mic.--My dear, I shall endeavor to do so to an unlimited extent! Ah, the sun has again risen--the clouds have passed--the sky is clear, and another score may be begun at the butcher's.--Heep, precede me. Emma, my love. *Au Revoir*.

(A gallant bow to Mrs. Micawber.)

A SCENE FROM DAVID COPPERFIELD.

CHARACTERS.

OLD FISHERMAN PEGGOTTY,

HAM PEGGOTTY,

DAVID COPPERFIELD.

Introduction.--The scene is the interior of the "Old Ark"; the time
is evening. The rain is falling outside, yet inside the old ark all is
snug and comfortable. The fire is burning brightly on the hearth, and
Mother Gummidge sits by it knitting. Ham has gone out to fetch little
Em'ly home from her work,--and the old fisherman sits smoking his
evening pipe by the table near the window. They are expecting Steerforth
and Copperfield in to spend the evening. Presently a knock is heard and
David enters. Old Peggotty gets up to greet him.

Old Peg.--Why! It's Mas'r Davy? Glad to see you, Mas'r Davy, you're
the first of the lot! Take off that cloak of yours if it's wet and draw
right up to the fire. Don't you mind Mawther Gummidge, Mas'r Davy; she's
a-thinkin' of the old 'un. She allers do be thinkin of the old 'un when
there's a storm a-comin' up, along of his havin' been drowned at sea.
Well, now, I must go and light up accordin' to custom. (He lights a
candle and puts it on the table by the window.) Theer we are! Theer we

are! A-lighted up accordin' to custom. Now, Mas'r Davy, you're a-wonderin'
what that little candle is for, ain't yer? Well, I'll tell yer. It's for
my little Em'ly. You see, the path ain't o'er light or cheerful arter
dark, so when I'm home here along the time that Little Em'ly comes home
from her work, I allers lights the little candle and puts it there on the
table in the winder, and it serves two purposes,--first, Em'ly sees it and
she says: "Theer's home," and likewise, "Theer's Uncle," fur if I ain't
here I never have no light showed. Theer! Now you're laughin' at me, Mas'r
Davy! You're a sayin' as how I'm a babby. Well, I don't know but I am.
(Walks towards table.) Not a babby to look at, but a babby to
consider on. A babby in the form of a Sea Porky-pine.

See the candle sparkle! I can hear it say--"Em'ly's lookin' at me! Little
Em'ly's comin'!" Right I am for here she is! (He goes to the door to
meet her; the door opens and Ham comes staggering in.)

Ham.--She's gone! Her that I'd a died fur, and will die fur even
now! She's gone!

Peggotty.--Gone!!

Ham.--Gone! She's run away! And think how she's run away when I
pray my good and gracious God to strike her down dead, sooner than let her
come to disgrace and shame.

Peggotty.--Em'ly gone! I'll not believe it. I must have
proof--proof.

Ham.--Read that writin'.

Peggotty.--No! I won't read that writin'--read it you, Mas'r Davy.
Slow, please. I don't know as I can understand.

David.--(Reads) "When you see this I shall be far away."

Peggotty.--Stop theer, Mas'r Davy! Stop theer! Fur away! My Little
Em'ly fur away! Well?

David.--(Reads) "Never to come back again unless he brings
me back a lady. Don't remember, Ham, that we were to be married, but try
to think of me as if I had died long ago, and was buried somewhere. My
last love and last tears for Uncle."

Peggotty.--Who's the man? What's his name? I want to know the man's
name.

Ham.--It warn't no fault of yours, Mas'r Davy, that I know.

Peggotty.--What! You don't mean his name's Steerforth, do you?

Ham.--Yes! His name is Steerforth, and he's a cursed villain!

Peggotty.--Where's my coat? Give me my coat! Help me on with it,
Mas'r Davy. Now bear a hand theer with my hat.

David.--Where are you going, Mr. Peggotty?

Peggotty.--I'm a goin' to seek fur my little Em'ly. First, I'm
going to stave in that theer boat and sink it where I'd a drownded him, as
I'm a living soul; if I'd a known what he had in him! I'd a drownded him,
and thought I was doin' right! Now I'm going to seek fur my Little Em'ly
throughout the wide wurrety!

A SCENE FROM THE SHAUGHRAUN.

Introduction.--This scene introduces the following characters:--Conn, the Shaughraun, a reckless, devil-may-care, true-hearted young vagabond, who is continually in a scrape from his desire to help a friend and his love of fun; his mother, Mrs. O'Kelly; his sweetheart, Moya Dolan, niece of the parish priest.

It is evening. Moya is alone in the kitchen. She has just put the kettle on the fire when Mrs. O'Kelly, Conn's mother, enters.

Mrs. O'K.--Is it yourself, Moya? I've come to see if that vagabond of mine has been around this way.

Moya.--Why should he be here, Mrs. O'Kelly? Hasn't he a home of his own?

Mrs. O'K.--The Shebeen is his home when he is not in jail. His father died o' drink, and Conn will go the same way.

Moya.--I thought your husband was drowned at sea?

Mrs. O'K.--And bless him, so he was.

Moya.--Well, that's a quare way o' dying o' drink.

Mrs. O'K.--The best of men he was, when he was sober--a betther never drhawed the breath o' life.

Moya.--But you say he never was sober.

Mrs. O'K.--Niver! An' Conn takes afther him!

Moya.--Mother, I'm afeared I shall take afther Conn.

Mrs. O'K.--Heaven forbid, and purtect you agin him! You a good dacent gurl, and desarve the best of husbands.

Moya.--Them's the only ones that gets the worst. More betoken yoursilf, Mrs. O'Kelly.

Mrs. O'K.--Conn niver did an honest day's work in his life--but dhrinkin' and fishin', an' shootin', an' sportin', and love-makin'.

Moya.--Sure, that's how the quality pass their lives.

Mrs. O'K.--That's it. A poor man that sports the sowl of a gintleman is called a blackguard.

(At this moment Conn appears in the doorway.)

Conn.--(At left.) Some one is talkin' about me! Ah, Moya, Darlin', come here. (Business as if he reached out his hands to Moya as he comes forward to meet her, and passes her over to his left so he seems to stand in center between Moya on left and Mrs. O'Kelly on right.) Was the old Mother thryin' to make little o' me? Don't you belave a word that comes out o' her! She's jealous o' me. (Laughing as he shakes his finger at his mother.) Yes, ye are! You're chokin' wid it this very minute! Oh, Moya darlin', she's jealous to see my two arms about ye. But she's proud o' me. Oh, she's proud o' me as an old him that's got a duck for a chicken. Howld your whist now Mother! Wipe your mouth and give me a kiss.

Mrs. O'K.--Oh, Conn, what have you been afther? The polls have been in the cabin today about ye. They say you stole Squire Foley's horse.

Conn.--Stole his horse! Sure the baste is safe and sound in his paddock this minute.

Mrs. O'K.--But he says you stole it for the day to go huntin'?

Conn.--Well, here's a purty thing, for a horse to run away wid a man's characther like this! Oh, Wurra! may I never die in sin, but this was the way of it. I was standin' by owld Foley's gate, whin I heard the cry of the hounds coming across the tail of the bog, an' there they wor, my dear, spread out like the tail of a paycock, an' the finest dog fox ye ever seen a sailin' ahead of thim up the boreen, and right across the churchyard. It was enough to raise the inhabitints out of the ground! Well, as I looked, who should come and put her head over the gate besoide me but the Squire's brown mare, small blame to her. Divil a word I said to her, nor she to me, for the hounds had lost their scent, we knew by their yelp and whine as they hunted among the gravestones. When, whist! the fox went by us. I leapt upon the gate, an' gave a shriek of a view-halloo to the whip; in a minute the pack caught the scent again, an' the whole field came roaring past.

The mare lost her head entoirely and tore at the gate. "Stop," says I, "ye divil!" an' I slipt a taste of a rope over her head an' into her mouth. Now mind the cunnin' of the baste, she was quiet in a minute. "Come home, now," ses I. "aisy!" an' I threw my leg across her.

Be jabbers! No sooner was I on her back than--Whoo! Holy Rocket! she was over the gate, an' tearin' afther the hounds loike mad. "Yoicks!" ses I; "Come back you thafe of the world, where you takin' me to?" as she carried me through the huntin' field, an' landed me by the soide of the masther of the hounds, Squire Foley himself.

He turned the color of his leather breeches.

"Mother o'Moses!" ses he, "Is that Conn, the Shaughraun, on my brown mare?"

"Bad luck to me!" ses I, "It's no one else!"

"You sthole my horse," ses the Squire.

"That's a lie!" ses I, "for it was your horse sthole me!"

Moya.--(Laughing.) And what did he say to that, Conn?

Conn.--I couldn't stop to hear, Moya, for just then we took a stone wall together an' I left him behind in the ditch.

Mrs. O'K.--You'll get a month in jail for this.

Conn.--Well, it was worth it.

BOUCICAULT.

The Codes Of Hammurabi And Moses
W. W. Davies

QTY

The discovery of the Hammurabi Code is one of the greatest achievements of archaeology, and is of paramount interest, not only to the student of the Bible, but also to all those interested in ancient history...

Religion   **ISBN:** *1-59462-338-4*   **Pages:132**
MSRP $12.95

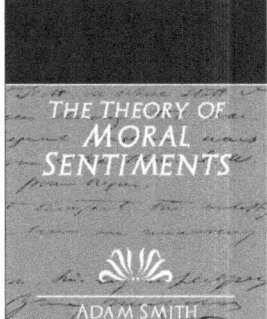

The Theory of Moral Sentiments
Adam Smith

QTY

This work from 1749. contains original theories of conscience amd moral judgment and it is the foundation for systemof morals.

Philosophy   **ISBN:** *1-59462-777-0*   **Pages:536**
MSRP $19.95

Jessica's First Prayer
Hesba Stretton

QTY

In a screened and secluded corner of one of the many railway-bridges which span the streets of London there could be seen a few years ago, from five o'clock every morning until half past eight, a tidily set-out coffee-stall, consisting of a trestle and board, upon which stood two large tin cans, with a small fire of charcoal burning under each so as to keep the coffee boiling during the early hours of the morning when the work-people were thronging into the city on their way to their daily toil...

Pages:84

Childrens   **ISBN:** *1-59462-373-2*   *MSRP $9.95*

My Life and Work
Henry Ford

QTY

Henry Ford revolutionized the world with his implementation of mass production for the Model T automobile. Gain valuable business insight into his life and work with his own auto-biography... "We have only started on our development of our country we have not as yet, with all our talk of wonderful progress, done more than scratch the surface. The progress has been wonderful enough but..."

Pages:300

Biographies/   **ISBN:** *1-59462-198-5*   *MSRP $21.95*

The Art of Cross-Examination
Francis Wellman

QTY

I presume it is the experience of every author, after his first book is published upon an important subject, to be almost overwhelmed with a wealth of ideas and illustrations which could readily have been included in his book, and which to his own mind, at least, seem to make a second edition inevitable. Such certainly was the case with me; and when the first edition had reached its sixth impression in five months, I rejoiced to learn that it seemed to my publishers that the book had met with a sufficiently favorable reception to justify a second and considerably enlarged edition. ..

Reference   ISBN: *1-59462-647-2*

Pages:412

MSRP $19.95

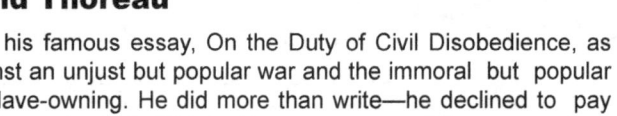

On the Duty of Civil Disobedience
Henry David Thoreau

QTY

Thoreau wrote his famous essay, On the Duty of Civil Disobedience, as a protest against an unjust but popular war and the immoral but popular institution of slave-owning. He did more than write—he declined to pay his taxes, and was hauled off to gaol in consequence. Who can say how much this refusal of his hastened the end of the war and of slavery ?

Law   ISBN: *1-59462-747-9*

Pages:48

MSRP $7.45

Dream Psychology Psychoanalysis for Beginners
Sigmund Freud

QTY

Sigmund Freud, born Sigismund Schlomo Freud (May 6, 1856 - September 23, 1939), was a Jewish-Austrian neurologist and psychiatrist who co-founded the psychoanalytic school of psychology. Freud is best known for his theories of the unconscious mind, especially involving the mechanism of repression; his redefinition of sexual desire as mobile and directed towards a wide variety of objects; and his therapeutic techniques, especially his understanding of transference in the therapeutic relationship and the presumed value of dreams as sources of insight into unconscious desires.

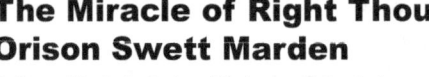

Psychology   ISBN: *1-59462-905-6*

Pages:196

MSRP $15.45

The Miracle of Right Thought
Orison Swett Marden

QTY

Believe with all of your heart that you will do what you were made to do. When the mind has once formed the habit of holding cheerful, happy, prosperous pictures, it will not be easy to form the opposite habit. It does not matter how improbable or how far away this realization may see, or how dark the prospects may be, if we visualize them as best we can, as vividly as possible, hold tenaciously to them and vigorously struggle to attain them, they will gradually become actualized, realized in the life. But a desire, a longing without endeavor, a yearning abandoned or held indifferently will vanish without realization.

Self Help   ISBN: *1-59462-644-8*

Pages:360

MSRP $25.45

The Rosicrucian Cosmo-Conception Mystic Christianity *by Max Heindel*　　ISBN: *1-59462-188-8*　**$38.95**
The Rosicrucian Cosmo-conception is not dogmatic, neither does it appeal to any other authority than the reason of the student. It is: not controversial, but is: sent forth in the, hope that it may help to clear...　　New Age/Religion Pages 646

Abandonment To Divine Providence *by Jean-Pierre de Caussade*　　ISBN: *1-59462-228-0*　**$25.95**
"The Rev. Jean Pierre de Caussade was one of the most remarkable spiritual writers of the Society of Jesus in France in the 18th Century. His death took place at Toulouse in 1751. His works have gone through many editions and have been republished...　　Inspirational/Religion Pages 400

Mental Chemistry *by Charles Haanel*　　ISBN: *1-59462-192-6*　**$23.95**
Mental Chemistry allows the change of material conditions by combining and appropriately utilizing the power of the mind. Much like applied chemistry creates something new and unique out of careful combinations of chemicals the mastery of mental chemistry...　　New Age Pages 354

The Letters of Robert Browning and Elizabeth Barret Barrett 1845-1846 vol II　　ISBN: *1-59462-193-4*　**$35.95**
by Robert Browning and Elizabeth Barrett　　Biographies Pages 596

Gleanings In Genesis (volume I) *by Arthur W. Pink*　　ISBN: *1-59462-130-6*　**$27.45**
Appropriately has Genesis been termed "the seed plot of the Bible" for in it we have, in germ form, almost all of the great doctrines which are afterwards fully developed in the books of Scripture which follow...　　Religion/Inspirational Pages 420

The Master Key *by L. W. de Laurence*　　ISBN: *1-59462-001-6*　**$30.95**
In no branch of human knowledge has there been a more lively increase of the spirit of research during the past few years than in the study of Psychology, Concentration and Mental Discipline. The requests for authentic lessons in Thought Control, Mental Discipline and...　　New Age/Psychology Pages 422

The Lesser Key Of Solomon Goetia *by L. W. de Laurence*　　ISBN: *1-59462-092-X*　**$9.95**
This translation of the first book of the "Lernegton" which is now for the first time made accessible to students of Talismanic Magic was done, after careful collation and edition, from numerous Ancient Manuscripts in Hebrew, Latin, and French...　　New Age/Occult Pages 92

Rubaiyat Of Omar Khayyam *by Edward Fitzgerald*　　ISBN:*1-59462-332-5*　**$13.95**
Edward Fitzgerald, whom the world has already learned, in spite of his own efforts to remain within the shadow of anonymity, to look upon as one of the rarest poets of the century, was born at Bredfield, in Suffolk, on the 31st of March, 1809. He was the third son of John Purcell...　　Music Pages 172

Ancient Law *by Henry Maine*　　ISBN: *1-59462-128-4*　**$29.95**
The chief object of the following pages is to indicate some of the earliest ideas of mankind, as they are reflected in Ancient Law, and to point out the relation of those ideas to modern thought.　　Religiom/History Pages 452

Far-Away Stories *by William J. Locke*　　ISBN: *1-59462-129-2*　**$19.45**
"Good wine needs no bush, but a collection of mixed vintages does. And this book is just such a collection. Some of the stories I do not want to remain buried for ever in the museum files of dead magazine-numbers an author's not unpardonable vanity..."　　Fiction Pages 272

Life of David Crockett *by David Crockett*　　ISBN: *1-59462-250-7*　**$27.45**
"Colonel David Crockett was one of the most remarkable men of the times in which he lived. Born in humble life, but gifted with a strong will, an indomitable courage, and unremitting perseverance...　　Biographies/New Age Pages 424

Lip-Reading *by Edward Nitchie*　　ISBN: *1-59462-206-X*　**$25.95**
Edward B. Nitchie, founder of the New York School for the Hard of Hearing, now the Nitchie School of Lip-Reading, Inc, wrote "LIP-READING Principles and Practice". The development and perfecting of this meritorious work on lip-reading was an undertaking...　　How-to Pages 400

A Handbook of Suggestive Therapeutics, Applied Hypnotism, Psychic Science　　ISBN: *1-59462-214-0*　**$24.95**
by Henry Munro　　Health/New Age/Health/Self-help Pages 376

A Doll's House: and Two Other Plays *by Henrik Ibsen*　　ISBN: *1-59462-112-8*　**$19.95**
Henrik Ibsen created this classic when in revolutionary 1848 Rome. Introducing some striking concepts in playwriting for the realist genre, this play has been studied the world over.　　Fiction/Classics/Plays 308

The Light of Asia *by sir Edwin Arnold*　　ISBN: *1-59462-204-3*　**$13.95**
In this poetic masterpiece, Edwin Arnold describes the life and teachings of Buddha. The man who was to become known as Buddha to the world was born as Prince Gautama of India but he rejected the worldly riches and abandoned the reigns of power when...　　Religion/History/Biographies Pages 170

The Complete Works of Guy de Maupassant *by Guy de Maupassant*　　ISBN: *1-59462-157-8*　**$16.95**
"For days and days, nights and nights, I had dreamed of that first kiss which was to consecrate our engagement, and I knew not on what spot I should put my lips..."　　Fiction/Classics Pages 240

The Art of Cross-Examination *by Francis L. Wellman*　　ISBN: *1-59462-309-0*　**$26.95**
Written by a renowned trial lawyer, Wellman imparts his experience and uses case studies to explain how to use psychology to extract desired information through questioning.　　How-to/Science/Reference Pages 408

Answered or Unanswered? *by Louisa Vaughan*　　ISBN: *1-59462-248-5*　**$10.95**
Miracles of Faith in China　　Religion Pages 112

The Edinburgh Lectures on Mental Science (1909) *by Thomas*　　ISBN: *1-59462-008-3*　**$11.95**
This book contains the substance of a course of lectures recently given by the writer in the Queen Street Hail, Edinburgh. Its purpose is to indicate the Natural Principles governing the relation between Mental Action and Material Conditions...　　New Age/Psychology Pages 148

Ayesha *by H. Rider Haggard*　　ISBN: *1-59462-301-5*　**$24.95**
Verily and indeed it is the unexpected that happens! Probably if there was one person upon the earth from whom the Editor of this, and of a certain previous history, did not expect to hear again...　　Classics Pages 380

Ayala's Angel *by Anthony Trollope*　　ISBN: *1-59462-352-X*　**$29.95**
The two girls were both pretty, but Lucy who was twenty-one who supposed to be simple and comparatively unattractive, whereas Ayala was credited, as her Bombwhat romantic name might show, with poetic charm and a taste for romance. Ayala when her father died was nineteen...　　Fiction Pages 484

The American Commonwealth *by James Bryce*　　ISBN: *1-59462-286-8*　**$34.45**
An interpretation of American democratic political theory. It examines political mechanics and society from the perspective of Scotsman James Bryce　　Politics Pages 572

Stories of the Pilgrims *by Margaret P. Pumphrey*　　ISBN: *1-59462-116-0*　**$17.95**
This book explores pilgrims religious oppression in England as well as their escape to Holland and eventual crossing to America on the Mayflower, and their early days in New England...　　History Pages 268

QTY

The Fasting Cure by *Sinclair Upton*   ISBN: *1-59462-222-1* **$13.95**
In the Cosmopolitan Magazine for May, 1910, and in the Contemporary Review (London) for April, 1910, I published an article dealing with my experiences in fasting. I have written a great many magazine articles, but never one which attracted so much attention... New Age/Self Help/Health Pages 164

Hebrew Astrology by *Sepharial*   ISBN: *1-59462-308-2* **$13.45**
In these days of advanced thinking it is a matter of common observation that we have left many of the old landmarks behind and that we are now pressing forward to greater heights and to a wider horizon than that which represented the mind-content of our progenitors... Astrology Pages 144

Thought Vibration or The Law of Attraction in the Thought World   ISBN: *1-59462-127-6* **$12.95**
by *William Walker Atkinson*   *Psychology/Religion Pages 144*

Optimism by *Helen Keller*   ISBN: *1-59462-108-X* **$15.95**
Helen Keller was blind, deaf, and mute since 19 months old, yet famously learned how to overcome these handicaps, communicate with the world, and spread her lectures promoting optimism. An inspiring read for everyone... Biographies/Inspirational Pages 84

Sara Crewe by *Frances Burnett*   ISBN: *1-59462-360-0* **$9.45**
In the first place, Miss Minchin lived in London. Her home was a large, dull, tall one, in a large, dull square, where all the houses were alike, and all the sparrows were alike, and where all the door-knockers made the same heavy sound... Childrens/Classic Pages 88

The Autobiography of Benjamin Franklin by *Benjamin Franklin*   ISBN: *1-59462-135-7* **$24.95**
The Autobiography of Benjamin Franklin has probably been more extensively read than any other American historical work, and no other book of its kind has had such ups and downs of fortune. Franklin lived for many years in England, where he was agent... Biographies/History Pages 332

Name	
Email	
Telephone	
Address	
City, State ZIP	

☐ **Credit Card**   ☐ **Check / Money Order**

Credit Card Number	
Expiration Date	
Signature	

Please Mail to: Book Jungle
                    PO Box 2226
                    Champaign, IL 61825
or Fax to: *630-214-0564*

www.ingramcontent.com/pod-product-compliance
Lightning Source LLC
Chambersburg PA
CBHW08074725O626
47162CB00010B/3052